Dedicated to Paul and Heather

Bibliografische Information der Deutschen Nationalbibliothek: Die Deutsche Nationalbibliothek verzeichnet diese Publikation in der Deutschen Nationalbibliografie; detaillierte bibliografische Daten sind im Internet über dnb.dnb.de abrufbar.

© 2018 Tarek Waleed
Herstellung und Verlag: BoD – Books on Demand, Norderstedt

ISBN: 978-3-7481-4762-6

Table of Contents

1. How It is 1
2. The Evil City of Frankfurt 1
3. Uncle Murad Explains the World in Cairo 2
4. Cem and the Asteroid 4
5. Enter the Terror Sheikh 6
6. Planting the Seed 8
7. The Little Sheikh 13
8. Blood and honor 19
9. Credit Where Credit is Due 21
10. A Middle East conflict 22
11. The Gauland Twins 28
12. Why I like Jews 31

Just Before The 11th of September

1. The View from Paul and Heather 29
2. Robert Falcon Scott High 44
3. The Age of Dissent 45
4. Islam Act 47
5. Fundamentalism for Beginners 50
6. The Miller's Home Library 54
7. Kuffar Literature 59
8. This Machine Kills Fascists 61
9. Don't Tell It on the Mountain 65
10. Georgia Lynch Mob 70
11. Don't Let The Sun Set On Him Here 75
12. Sally Jefferson 77
13. Twenty Gods or None At All 80
14. Shahada 84

15. Paul's Birthday Present	86
16. The Morning after the Night Before	91
17. Homeward Bound	93

After the 11th of September

1. Future Legislators of Society	97
2. Trojan Horses	98
3. The Dark Ladies of Cairo	102
4. Here Comes the Judge	105
5. Frankfurt Railway Station	108
6. The Defense	114
7. Midnight Call to Georgia	120

MY PART IN 9/11

How It Is

Like the great Tom Paine once said: "These are the times that try men's souls." I, today, have come to believe that were it not for Tom and his compatriots— Jefferson, Madison, Franklin, the American Founding Fathers—that I would be either a dead, religious Muslim fanatic or not even born at all due to Nazi racist madness. A strange position for a German Arab of my generation to hold, you may think, but if you want to laugh in my face or kick me in the pants because of it, then bring it, bring it on, for this is where I stand.

But of course it wasn't always like that. We have all said or done things in our lives that we shame ourselves for even years and years later; but believe me, I have never heard of anyone the likes of me. Something so dumb and mean and stupid, so childish, evil, and hurtful to people who deserved a whole lot better and this all in connection with one of the most horrific crimes in human history. It was so bad that it took me the best part of 16 years to come crawling out of my hole where I hid myself to make some kind of amends. This is my tale.

The Evil City of Frankfurt

Call me Tarek. Tarek Waleed. I was born in Germany in Frankfurt am Main (that city of banks, greed, finance and drugs) at the beginning of the 1980s of German and Egyptian parents. I grew up there, in the borough of Bockenheim, a culturally mixed area. We lived on Falkstraße close to the university campus. As a child I used to sneak up on to the roof of our house and from there over the years I saw the skyline growing. I remember watching the trade tower being built: that huge obelisk with its shining pyramid on top and blinking light. This, said my Egyptian father, was the Eye of the Illuminati, the Jews, and the Freemasons. My German mom considered this to be just figments of his Arabic imagination, and I didn't know what to think.

When my dad was in his mid-40s, struggling with his midlife crisis, he decided to become a more radical type of Muslim. At that time, I was 9 years old and did not understand why Dad all of a sudden started to pray all over the living room at all times of day and night. I was wondering because I never saw him praying before. He was always running to the mosque and bringing people from there home—and not just his taxi driver colleagues as usual. When I asked him about it, he just said that he was finding his way back to his religion. I found this strange because I thought he always been a Muslim anyway. "Reverting," he called it. My mom said it was just his way of dealing with getting old. My sister and I found this all very confusing, standing between a Catholic mother and a hyper Sunni father. I didn't know then that this disturbance to my identity would one day lead to catastrophe.

Uncle Murad Explains the World in Cairo

Every year during the school summer vacation, we travelled to Egypt to visit Dad's family. We stayed at uncle Murad's place with his wife and two sons in Medinat Nasr, Cairo. As a child, Cairo seemed to me an incredible sleepless, noisy, hot, mysterious, and fantastical place. The capital of the world, the mother of all cities. The land of the Arabian nights. A place of dreams and miracles and fantasies.

I will never forget one evening when my chubby, hairy Uncle Murad explained the world to me. The rest of the family went out and we were alone together. I sat directly opposite to him on the sofa, he in a big, old-fashioned chair. Next to us was the television where he watched CNN greedily, 24 hours a day.

Turning to me, he said, "Tarek I have to talk to you. I know you come from Germany and there are maybe things that you haven't been told." He pointed at the television and said, "The Jews, the Jews in America."

"What do you mean, Uncle Murad?" I asked.

Uncle Murad lit a cigarette, blew out the smoke, and looked directly at me. "Listen, Habibi! This here," and he pointed again at the TV, "This here is all under the control of the Jews in the United States. They want to show the world that we Arabs are the bad guys. Because, Tarek, the Jews always controlled the US and told them what to do because they do everything in their power to control the whole world. I know this is a difficult subject for a little German boy, but I think you are old enough now to know these things."

Confused, I looked at the carpet and said, "But uncle, at school in Frankfurt I heard it different."

Uncle Murad laughed. "The Jews and the Americans, they want you to feel guilty and not to say what you think."

"How do you know all this Uncle Murad?"

Murad took a sip from his tea put his cup back on the table and began pacing the room.

"Do you really believe what the media tells you, Tarek? You grew up in Germany and you think you are free, but you are brainwashed everyday and you all are a bunch of puppets on a string."

He walked across to the window and closed it, shutting out the noise of the evening traffic and turning around, then said excitedly, "All Jewish lies. Hitler didn't kill six million Jews; he didn't kill no one. Tarek, you are not a little kid anymore, you have to know all those things. The Jewish clique of the World Bank and their Freemason friends like the Rothshilds from your Frankfurt run this planet."

He ran up to the television and went down on his knees, pointing at the screen with his finger, saying, "Tarek, the media is controlled by the Jews! Just look at this CNN. Who founded it?"

"I don't know!" I said, shocked at his manic behavior.

"Ted Turner! And what is he? A Jew! Or in Hollywood, you know them Warner Brothers? Who are they? Jews! Or this roaring lion before the movie, this Goldwyn Mayer. Jews! Or what's the name of this movie director, Goldberg or someone?"

"Steven Spielberg, Uncle," I said.

"Yes, exactly. Steven Spielberg. And what is he, Tarek? This Steven Spielberg?"

"A Jew, Uncle Murad."

"Exactly. You're learning, my boy," he said, smiling at me, obviously pleased.

I couldn't know then what a tragedy this type of instruction would lead me to one day.

Cem and the Asteroid

But, like always, there was another view of the world. A couple of weeks later back in Frankfurt, I was hanging out with my Turkish friend Cem who was the same age as me. We always liked to get as near as we could to this group of winos who gathered every day next to the observatory of the Senckenberg museum in Bockenheim to drink and fool around.

Cem had a shock of black curly hair so thick you could hardly see his face, always wore a Bayern Munich football shirt, and wanted to be a professional soccer player. Like me, he was born in Frankfurt but his parents came from Anatolia and I knew them both very well. And like the rest of his family, they were all great believers in the glory of the Ottoman Empire and the greatness of the Turkish nation. They were great haters of all Americans, like a lot of my family were.

As we were watching the antics of the street drunks (who were always good entertainment), Cem suddenly said to me, "You know what I saw on television last night? There was this documentary about asteroids and some of them real monsters come really close to the earth sometimes, and they are watching out for them all of the time because if one of the big ones were to hit the earth it would be the end of us all—like when the dinosaurs were wiped out by one millions of years ago."

I looked up at the observatory in front of us and into the sky beyond. This was pretty frightening stuff.

"And you know what I thought, Tarek? If one of them, a real planet-killer, was really heading towards us on a collision course, the whole world would as one would jump up and say, 'Where are the Americans? The Americans must save us. What are the Americans going to do?' No one, nowhere, anywhere, would be asking, 'What are the Turks going to do?'"

I burst out laughing. "No, Tarek! Seriously, it was suddenly completely clear to me, those are the guys you can rely on with something like that. I mean, only they can take on a job like that. I mean, who else? Didn't they invent the washing machine and send the first man to the moon? Whatshisname? Louis Armstrong. So, if an asteroid was coming at us, like that they'd set some of their real brainy science Yahudis on to it, like Richard Dreyfuss in Close Encounters and Jaws."

"You mean, Cem, the whole world would think that only the Americans could save us?" I asked doubtfully.

"Of this I am quite certain," said Cem.

I noticed that the group of street drunks had stopped drinking and fooling around and were looking across at us strangely.

"Cem, if those guys over there tell your father what you have been saying, he'll kill you."

"Evet," said Cem.

If only I had listened to Cem, perhaps nothing of that terrible thing would later have happened.

Enter The Terror Sheikh

There was a man in my neighborhood in Bockenheim who went from house to house collecting donations; he said it was for poor orphans in Palestine. It turned out later he was actually collecting money for terrorist attacks, which means the killing of the nonbelievers, the "Kuffar." He spent a lot of time in the mosques in and around Frankfurt and also tried to recruit young people for the Jihad, fishing for lost souls. And one day he was standing in front of our house door.

I'd been talking to my mom, asking about Dad's midlife crisis and if it was a very serious disease. Mum said, "He just thinks a little bit more than usual. Nothing to worry about." But Dad had really changed over the last few months. He was constantly in a bad mood and agitated, always reading his Quran, and spent more time in the mosque than driving his cab and earning his living. It was as if he really had rediscovered the religion that he had given up on soon after arriving in Germany as a young guy, and learning the pleasures of the decadent, western Kuffar life. But then came age and family, responsibility, and a routine, badly paid job, and his illusions of success, wealth, rich women, expensive cars, and gold on the street in the Promised Land evaporated quickly. Like a lot of others, disappointed Muslims sought comfort in the Quran and Islam and a late recognition of their moral supremacy over the rotten and sinful West.

And that's how religion came into our home. My mom's pride and joy as a kindergarten teacher was her library of used books that she had bought over the years here and there. One day, my dad came home in a religious fury shouting, "Sophy, those books have got to go, throw them out! They just take up space and gather dust and all we need to read is in the holy Quran."
My mom reared up. I had never seen her so angry: "Just like you burned the library at Alexandria or what? You Muslim hero? Over my dead body!" And then she walked out, slamming the door. They didn't speak for days. I guess in that silent house I felt a real intimation of the Clash of Civilizations.
The doorbell rang, and I walked across and opened the door. I could hear him wheezing for breath before I saw him: a mysterious collector for Palestinian orphans. He wore a sort of turban on his head and seemed to be wrapped in bedsheets and a big brushy beard that went down his waist. He just stood there, wheezing and grunting and snorting as I stared at him in fear. His left eye was snow-white and the right one mad and gleaming.

"Hello, Tarek! I am a friend of your father. My name is Hamed. I have a meeting with your dad today."

All in all, I didn't have a really good feeling about this character.

My father came up behind me, his arms stretched out before him. "Abu Hamed, how are you, brother? Welcome to my home."

At the same time my mom came along the hallway, and my father, full of joy, said, "Sophy, look who is here to visit us. Brother Hamed!"

My mother simply said, "Why doesn't that surprise me?" and walked straight by, out of the house.

My father, obviously embarrassed, pushed me forward, saying, "Brother Hamed, this is my son Tarek.

Say hello to Uncle Hamed, he is a wise and pious and learned man."

"Hello, Uncle Hamed," I managed to say before being engulfed in a bear hug by the monster in front of me. I wanted to throw up.

"Go and bring tea for our guest, my son," my father said before they disappeared into the living room. I brought them their tea and they sent me away, spending the next two hours alone in whispered conversation.

Planting the Seed

In the following weeks he visited us often and my mother always absented herself when he arrived. I had the impression she was worried about me somehow but couldn't really do anything. Their conspirative meetings went on for a couple of weeks and my father becoming weirder and weirder. Then one day I was invited in as well to listen as the sheikh talked for hours and hours about the wonders of Islam and how it would triumph over the entire world and how the unbelievers would be defeated and burnt in hell.

I began to find it all fascinating. It seemed to be a real explanation for everything and I could understand my father's commitment. Not long after, I became a member of a small group of young disciples centered around Sheikh Hamed.

The Friday prayers were over, and Sheikh Hamed, Muaviz, Ehup, and I went out to eat near our backyard mosque in the Galluswarte, in a kebab shop run by one of the brothers. It was pouring rain and the three of us ran behind the fat, puffing sheikh through the grubby streets till we were there. As we ran I noticed his brand new "Air Jordans" beneath his voluminous robes.

My mother was troubled, to say the least, that I was spending so much time in this company, but my father insisted that I needed this Islamic education. Ehup and Muaviz were two brothers whose parents came from Turkey and they were always following the sheikh around—they absolutely hero-worshipped him. Ehup was 16 years of age and had a fluffy little beard and had already been in big trouble with the law. His brother, Muaviz, was two years younger, had no beard at all, and was an even nastier piece of work. Both always wore black clothes, had black hair, and even blacker fantasies.

We ordered at the counter and sat ourselves down. The sheikh began to speak: "It is good, brothers, that we eat in this good Islamic eating place because if you eat in a devil's place like that," he said, pointing out of the window at a McDonald's on the other side of the street. "Wallah, every cent goes to the Zionist in Israel and the Zionist are like Satan, all of them child murderers!" The two brothers next to me nodded simultaneously in agreement.

"Tarek, habibi," continued the sheikh, "Did you ever look at the Coca-Cola logo in the mirror?"

"No," I said curiously.

"You would read in Arabic that there is no God."

"No, I didn't know that, Sheikh Hamed."

"You must know, Tarek, that the Jews in America always work with secret signs and symbols. They conceal themselves in order to perpetrate their evil plans. Did you ever see the Eye in the pyramid on the American dollar? The symbol of the Jewish Freemasons just like the filthy trade tower here in Frankfurt. The Freemasons and the Jews, they control the world from America. It is all in the protocols of Zion."

The waitress, an attractive girl who was wearing an expensive silk headscarf, came over with our food. I smiled at her and said, "thank you," but she simply looked away and went without speaking. I noticed that Sheikh Hamed was staring at me angrily. He then turned and said to Ehup and Muaviz, "very good, my brothers. I noticed that you did not look at the woman; your eyes were fixed at the floor. Alhamdulillah, this is how it should be." He then turned and said to Ehup and Muaviz, "very good, my brothers. I noticed that you did not look at the woman; your eyes were fixed at the floor. Alhamdulillah, this is how it should be." Then, he turned back to me, saying, "You must know, my son, that temptation lurks everywhere. Do you not believe in Shaitan and the evil amongst the Jinn and how they numb our senses with poisonous thoughts and lead us to the fires of hell where the Kuffar suffer forever?"

"Allah protect us," said Ehup and Muaviz together.

I looked out of the window at the traffic passing by on the street outside, and with my nine years, felt a mixture of fear for eternity and guilt for my weakness.

"This also, Tarek, applies not just to women and their wiles but also to basketball, music, dancing, singing, football, skateboarding, film, and television, and all the things that are pleasing to the Kuffar. Curse them!"

I didn't understand what was so wrong with those things but I didn't have the courage to say anything against him. We carried on eating. Then, Ehup said, "Tarek, in the past I did many evil things: drugs, drinking, and fighting. I was a bad example for my brother, Allah forgive me, but thanks to Sheikh Hamed I am back on the straight path, Alhamdulillah."

"No, habibi, Allah alone brought you back to the
straight path, the Sirat al Mustakeen."

"You are right, Sheikh Hamed, of course it was Allah," Ehup replied. "I really was a great sinner."

I was wondering what it was that a 16-year-old could have done that was so terrible when Muaviz broke in, saying, "Ehup, tell them about the thing with the horse."

Ehup looked over to me and said, "I think he is too young to hear that!"

But Sheikh Hamed said, "No, no, habibi, go ahead and tell, so that Tarek can understand what the holy Islam has made of you."

"Ok, Tarek," he began as the other two leaned back to listen, smiling. They had obviously heard the story before.

"When I was your age, Tarek, maybe a little bit older, my cousin and I used to go on our bikes in the night to a horse stable near to where we lived. A kuffar riding school for little girls."

"Yes, yes," gasped the sheikh, snapping for air.
"Now it comes." His eyes were wide with pleasure.

Ehup continued: "We then used to creep out to where the horses were standing sleeping in a field. They sleep while standing, these creatures, Tarek! Naturally, we brought something with us."

"What did you bring?" I asked.

"We each had a one-meter-long, thick wooden stick with lots of splinters on it."

The sheikh began to giggle in anticipation. "And do you know, Tarek, what we did then? My cousin puts one end of his stick in the rear end of one of them and I from behind rammed it with all my strength. Bang! Right into it." The three of them roared with laughter.

I simply sat there looking at them. Then, the sheikh said, "What's wrong, Tarek? It was only an animal." He looked over to Ehup and said, "Ehup, why don't you tell Tarek your other story about chopping the lamb after Ramadan?"

Ehup smiled and said, "Ok," and his brother, Muaviz, laughing, said, "This is great, here it comes."

"Two days before the end of Ramadan, my father bought a lamb to sacrifice for the feast. He put it in a cage in the cellar of our house and we kids used to go down there and torture it a bit. One night I had it alone all for myself and I took a can of orange spray and sprayed it all over orange because prisoners wear orange, you understand Tarek, I wanted my very own personal prisoner. I had a knitting needle from my mom with me. You know, its eyes just popped like grapes."

"But what did your father say?" I asked in horror.

Muaviz answered for his brother, saying, "When dad saw the blinded lamb, he realized that even though Ehup was only 12, he had what it takes, so he let him cut the lamb's throat in the bathtub the next day himself."

"My cousin held its legs," said Ehup, "and I slit its throat, but I swear to God, Tarek, I wanted to cut its whole head off, its whole kuffar head."

All three once more began to roar with laughter. So loud that the whole room looked across to us and then resumed eating, stuffing great wads and chunks of halal meat into their mouths, kuffars and believers both. I think this was the moment when it began—my lifelong aversion to eating dead flesh. The sheikh could hardly control himself laughing; his big, fat belly was heaving to and fro. "Alhamdulillah, alhamdulillah," he kept saying, almost choking, and Ehup and Muaviz joined in, "Alhamdulillah, alhamdulillah," and the sheikh looked across at both of them with a secret smile in his eyes, as if he was thinking he found the right recruits at last. Me, he didn't even look at. Years later I read in a Frankfurt newspaper that all three of them who were sitting there with me that day had been killed in a drone attack in Afghanistan. Alhamdulillah. Yet had he known what would happen in another continent far away, I think that, despite everything, the sheikh would have been proud of his pupil Tarek. The devil is a carnivore.

The Little Sheikh

Little Mohammed was already very sick when he came to Frankfurt to visit us. My father had in the meantime reinvented himself professionally and next to his job as taxi driver begun to work as a guide for medical tourists from the Gulf states, ferrying them around during their stay in Germany.

As I was free from school at that time, I was able to go with my dad to the airport to pick up the family Said from New York City. This was a big deal because the family Said was a sort of Kuwaiti aristocrat family who lived in New York and so little Mohammed with his 13 years of age was like a genuine little prince.

"Take that gum out of your mouth," said my father as we were waiting in the reception area. So I went across and spat it out in the trash can. We didn't have to wait long for the Saids, and you couldn't miss them. I saw a group of people and a little kid sitting in a wheelchair. One of them was wearing a black niqab.

"Welcome to Germany," said my father lavishly, like Germany belonged to him.

"Hello Farouk, how are you?" answered Yassir, and they all began to kiss each other.

"That's my son Tarek. Say hello, Tarek!" said my father.

"Salam aleikum," I answered, to the best of my Arabic knowledge.

"Wa aleikum Salam, Tarek," said Yassir.

Yassir was about 1.60 m tall and a really small-sized guy. He reminded me of our Pakistani friend Billy who ran the Sicilian pizzeria at the Galluswarte. Like Billy, he was half-bald.

"This is my son, Mohammed," said Yasser.

Little Mohammed, because of his cancer, looked very weak—

so weak that he had to sit in a wheelchair. He was very thin and despite his dark skin looked pale. He was wearing a black jogging suitand a New York Yankees baseball cap. My father bent over to Mohammed in the wheelchair and asked, "How are you, Mohammed?"

"Alhamdulillah!" answered Mohammed with a weak voice. Then Yassir introduced his wife, Noor. The woman in the niqab didn't offer her hand but nodded to each of us.

"Hello," said Noor, but nothing else, like she didn't want to undermine Yassir's authority. Although standing next to her shrimp of a husband, Noor in her black clothing looked like a giant killer whale.

"You Tarek?" she asked.

"Yes," I answered nervously.

"Your dad has told me a lot about you," she said, her eyes grinning.

"I am Noor Mo's mother," she said, pointing at Mo with her thumb. She reeked really strongly of perfume.

"Welcome, all of you, to Germany," said my father again, this time a little slimily.

As we all walked out of the airport terminal, I heard Noor, who was trailing behind, muttering, "Germany, Germany boring!"

We drove from the Rhein-Main airport downtown to the Marriott Hotel, where the Saids were to check into the luxury suite that they rented for the rest of their visit. The Marriott was also close to the Frankfurt University Hospital, where little Mohammed would be getting his treatment. Our route led us along the Stresemann Allee through Sachsenhausen and then over the river Main so that they could see the skyline like my father had planned. The high towers of the banks, which he usually always told me are controlled by the Freemasons and Jews, were good enough today to give his guests a feeling of the German economic metropol of Frankfurt. He always did that anyway when family and friends were visiting him from Egypt, to show them that he made it big in a rich, western country. I don't think he liked what Noor let out when we were waiting at the red light. "What a tiny little village this Frankfurt is, everything is so small."

We arrived at the Marriott Hotel and the uniformed kuffar flunkeys came scuttling over to carry our bags. A couples of minutes later we were all packed into an elevator, and suddenly Noor lifted her niqab over her head clean of her body like it was a total body condom.

"Kurwa masz!!!" she swore, and looked at us all in disgust. "Don't they have air conditioning here? What's this for a primitive hole?" she asked her husband. She really blew us all away. And then looking at her I realized that the woman under the niqab didn't look like a woman from Kuwait. She had blond hair, piercing green eyes, and was wearing blue jeans and cowboy boots. Not only that, but a tight, red pullover that enhanced her enormous breasts, and hanging in between was a large silver cross with a man with long hair and a beard nailed to it. I began to suspect that Noor was probably not an Islamic Arabic lady on account of her looking more like a Frankfurt hooker. Later, driving from the Marriott home to Bockenheim, my dad told me who Noor really was.

Noor was a cover name for a Polish woman called Magda. Magda was a lady from London who Yassir had an affair with, an affair with consequences. Yassir had been having problems with his numberone wife and was quite sexually frustrated, so he sought relief in the London nightlife scene. One night as he was cruising around with his Arab buddies, he got to know Magda in a nightclub. Magda at that time was a well-known Shepherd's Bush call girl and extremely interested in all sorts of men with big, bulging pocketbooks.

Then, of course, one day she tells him that she is expecting a child from him, this being little Mo. For Yassir this was quite a problem, especially in regard to the reaction of his more than extremely religious family clan in Kuwait, and this with a Polish lady of the London night. Magda was over the moon with joy, but Yassir lost half his hair overnight through fright and fear of the Sharia. Magda told him the only way out was for them to marry, so Yassir, weak as he was, made her his wife number two. And before she could know it, she had a sack over her head and a ring on her finger. And Yassir was spared being stoned to death. But his problems were only beginning because he needed to get Magda into (Islamic) line. Wearing a niqab wouldn't be enough; she had to become a Muslim. But she swore that she would never give up the Catholic faith of Poland because Magda was the proudest Polish woman you can imagine, and obstinate as granite— like the Polish army at the gates of Vienna, like the Warsaw uprising, like the solidarity movement. And to press her point home, she beat him around the room with an ashtray.

After a couple of days Magda had the idea that I should visit Mo in the hospital because he had no one of his age to talk to in English. So I went along. It was already dark when my mum brought me there with the car. As I entered his hospital room I had a really bad feeling because I realized now how sick he really was. It was the first time I had been in contact with somebody so badly ill, and I was afraid that it might be contagious.

"Hi Tarek, how you doing? Come on in!" said Mo with his nasally New York accent.

Shyly, I entered the room, which was only lit by the harsh lamp light next to Mo's bed, which was next to a window facing the night skyline of Frankfurt. Through habit, I squinted my eyes, trying to see the Jews and Freemasons in the lit windows of the bank houses.

"Hi Mo, I am fine. How are you?"

"Alhamdulillah" answered Mo.

"What does that mean?"

"Thanks be to God. Didn't you know that?"

"Yeah, maybe, but I guess I forgot it."

Mo looked at me a while. "Tarek, you a Muslim or not?"

"Yeah, sure, but…"

"But? It's not that difficult. Yes or no?"

I sat on the side of his bed and said, "I don't know, I can't say. You know, since this guy, this weird sheikh's been coming around our house, I don't know what to think anymore."

Mo shifted himself up on his pillow. "What did he do?"

"It's what he said…you know, like…all people who don't accept Islam go to Hell and burn, like my mother, my sister and all my German friends from soccer here in Frankfurt. If that's Islam, Mo, I'm out!"

"Listen, Tarek," said Mo, "forget the clown. Guys who talk like that, they're enemies of Islam, not friends. Let me ask you something: What's the most important thing in a person's life?"

I simply shrugged.

"To do good things! Do you really think that a Jihadist who kills people like flies is loved by Allah in comparison to, say, a doctor who tries to save lives, like they're trying to do with mine here? Who do you think Allah is proud of? Sometimes I get the feeling that some Muslims are just into a type of death cult. That has nothing to do with true Islam. They just seem to want to kill people. A woman has a love affair… death sentence. You leave Islam because you can't believe anymore…death sentence. You joke about the prophet…death sentence. A man loves a man…death sentence. And even for thinking like this…death sentence. Is that what Allah wants, Tarek?"

Mo tried to sit up.

"Listen, Tarek," he said, leaning towards me. "Someone once said 'My country is the world and my religion to do good'…I think it was an English guy, Tom Paine, one of the Founding Fathers." Exhausted, he laid back on the pillow and with eyes fixed on the ceiling: "Only Allah can decide when life begins and ends; not men." And I saw the pain in his face. I realized that the cancer treatment must be really hard on him at his age.

"Listen, Tarek," he said after a while. "I believe that Allah wants lots of different ideas on the earth, that's what pleases him really. Says so in the Quran. I heard at school in New York that Thomas Jefferson said something like that too…a thousand religions… each as good as each other."

A nurse opened the door to the room, looked inside, saw us together, smiled, and closed the door.

"Tarek, when I am in Kuwait, the monotony of the place puts me to sleep. Although I'm from there, there is no individuality there. Everyone prays, wears the same clothes, goes to the same festivals, and the muezzin sings five times a day. But when I am back in New York City, I'm wide awake again. Everywhere there are the wildest people: buskers, artists, business types, every race on earth. There is a buzz there, Tarek, on the streets, people running here and there full of life and love of life. And whether you are a Jew, a Muslim, a Sikh, a Voodooist, or Christian, what unites us? We are all Americans. I love the place!"

And then I asked him: "Hey Mo, when you're better and get out of here, what do you want to do with your life?"

He looked at me sadly in the eyes: "I wanna study Islam, Tarek, from all sides, and then I'll become an imam and use the advantages that I have in life to support and spread a reformed Islam, a positive message, that is acceptable to the coming 21st century. That's what I want to do, I think."

Three weeks later, Mo died in New York City. He would have howled in his grave if he knew what I did.

Blood and Honor

Deep in the night I woke up with a shock. I heard my dad screaming in the street outside. I ran out of the house to him; he was lying on the sidewalk in a pool of blood with a knife sticking out of his stomach. Two dark figures disappeared into the night. Luckily, he survived the emergency operation and recovered quickly. I was traumatized I guess for a long time and felt afraid. At that time I came to really understand the meaning of one single word; that word was "honor." A five-letter word that has done nothing but screwed the world up. Among Arabs like us, when the sense of honor is injured, it can lead to a load of killing. The problem is that everybody has his or her own definition of it. Some feel their honor to be injured when you insult their big toe, and others when you insult their mother. Usually it's the mother.

Apparently, what happened was that there had been some sort of argument between my dad and a couple of other cab drivers, two Iraqis—some nonsense about a parking place. Insult followed insult and it all ended in a fight on the street outside the railway station. Naturally, under the circumstances, lots of mothers got insulted, really badly insulted and the whole thing ended with my dad abandoning his taxi and getting chased by two, maybe three, Iraqi families through the midnight streets of Frankfurt till they caught him and knifed him outside our house. In this way, honor was satisfied. The next day at school I told my Afghan friend, Jabbar, what had happened, and he said that it would be normal in Afghanistan to take revenge. Not just normal but necessary; blood revenge was the

only way to react to this type of thing.
He was a thin, little guy and his eyes were wide open and burning. He was my best friend. And loyal. And despite his small size, tough as hell. He walked with a limp. He was someone you could rely on. If there was a fight amongst kids, he was always in the thick of it, whatever the odds. He always used to say, "We Muslims have to stick together, Tarek! Help your Muslim brothers first and the kuffar only sometimes."His family were Pashtun fighters.
"Tarek," he said to me on the lunch break, "we've got to take blood revenge against those that did that to your father, it's the only way, the Afghan way! We keep cool heads and we plan it perfectly." I could see that he meant well. He explained to me that if I
didn't take revenge, then the honor of my family would be like dirt on the street. "But," he said, "seeing as these Iraqis are fully grown men, we better wait a couple of years till we are big enough to take them out. This doesn't matter because revenge, as we say in Afghanistan, is a meal best eaten cold. Like with us in Afghanistan, a man gets up one morning and travels 100 miles through the land and arriving in another place, kills the grandson of the man who killed his grandfather 100 years ago. And the people say, 'My God, wasn't he impatient.'"
Jabbar then pointed across the school yard at Simon, a German friend of ours. "See that kuffar Simon over there? His mother cheated on his father and now they are having a divorce and the lawyers are sending letters back and forth about money and cars and stuff. In Afghanistan she wouldn't be demanding anything; in Afghanistan the cow would be dead. That, Tarek, is what we call tradition. These Germans don't know what that is. You are either a victim or a man of honor. Even my own sister, if she would have married a German, I would have slit her throat in the washbasin. Either the name of your family is in the gutter, or the whole of Bockenheim is in flames. Your choice, Tarek."

Credit Where Credit is Due

Because the attack on my father had upset me so much, I could hardly sleep at night, and when I did, I wet the bed. So my mom thought a change of scene would be a good idea and started to take me to her brother (my uncle, Uwe) a few miles south, in Heidelberg, on weekends. The Meyer's home was completely German—they even had a cuckoo clock on the wall. Here, I saw the whole of my mother's German family: my uncle Uwe, my auntie Beate, and their dog, John F. Kennedy. All of them drinking beer and eating spätzle. I felt like I was living in the middle of the Munich Oktoberfest. My uncle Uwe was the best uncle in the world. He was a stocky, red-faced man with a well-trimmed mustache, always laughing and loved to drink the local wine. He was a retired German Army officer and always used to say that the best time in German history was under the American occupation.

When we were all seated at the dining table, he would like to pronounce as if he was delivering judgement. Things like, "Tarek, my boy, without the Yanks all would be lost. Without the Americans we would all be Nazis or Stalinists. We wouldn't be sitting here now talking in German, we would all be speaking Russian and we would be speaking in whispers under the table," and he would take a big gulp of wine. "I know my boys in the German Army, The Bundeswehr, they're all nice kids, but compared to the Russians they're just military garbage. If the Russians would come, they would have to run crying to the Americans. And our civilians are worse, always singing pacifist songs and demonstrating against something or another, mostly the Yanks who are the only ones standing between them and the Bolshies. All in all, the whole of the German nation and Europe as well is just a pack of spoiled children. The Yanks do all the heavy lifting and we just whinge and whine. Do you understand, Tarek, they are the only ones that guarantee us our freedom," and he would bang his glass down on the table. Case dismissed!

I was so impressed by his speeches that when he took me to the US base in Heidelberg at the "Patrick- Henry-Village" for the German-American Volksfest, I bought with my pocket money a huge stars and stripes to hang out of my bedroom window in Frankfurt.

A Middle East Conflict

That evening, Uncle Uwe dropped me and my flag off back home in the Falkstraße, where he wasn't a welcome guest. The last thing he said with a laugh before driving away was, "Soldier, don't surrender the flag!"

I marched whistling up the stairs to our fourth-floor apartment, the stars and stripes in my hand. As I got into the apartment I saw my dad, who had recovered from his knifing, sitting with his fellow Middle Eastern cab driver colleagues watching soccer. My mother and the other women had been banished to the kitchen. On these evenings the Sharia ruled. The men in the room all looked at me and at the flag I was carrying rolled up in my hands, which was about 6 square feet big. I was really looking forward to hanging it out of my bedroom window, my own private Fort Alamo. The room smelled strongly of cigarettes and shisha smoke.

"Tarek, what's that you've got there?" asked my father.

"The US flag. Bought it in Heidelberg. Gonna hang it out of my window," I answered cockily, still high from my visit to Uwe.

All four men in the room looked at me in silence, as if they were a court of village elders high up in the mountains somewhere, considering the verdict on a tribal traitor. Like they might lynch me for soiling the family honor.

Next to my father was sitting his Palestinian friend, Tony, who was the only non-Muslim in the room, Tony being Roman Catholic. He was a big, fat man with a load of red hair and seemed somehow to look Irish—maybe a regressive crusader gene. He had a strange pi-

ping voice. He was originally from Bethlehem. All the others guys used to laugh at him and thought him a bit loony because for the last 10 years he'd been saying that early one morning, when he'd been sitting in his cab at Bockenheim market at the bottom of Leipzigerstraße, he had seen a vision of the Queen of Heaven, that the Holy Blessed Virgin Mary, the Mother of God, had appeared to him. Since then he had been trying to persuade the City of Frankfurt to build a chapel in accordance with Her wishes dedicated to Our Lady of Bockenheim (without success). Tony always used to say "The Catholic religion is the only one over the centuries which has been repeatedly confirmed, and that by reason of the hundreds of appearances of Our Lady."

Then there was Ali. Ali was a Shia Muslim from Iran, which my father said was just a sect. Ali's main characteristic was that he seldom spoke and just stared evilly at the people. He had a big, hooked nose; was thin as a rake; and on the little finger of his left hand, a long, long nail. I used to watch with fascination him picking his ears with it. Ali had a son the same age as me, who he'd named Djihad, and who I used to go around and play with sometimes. Ali had a real machine gun hidden in his cellar, which we get to see sometimes. When Ali used to get into arguments with my dad and the other guys on the taxi stand at the railway station about who were the greatest, biggest, strongest, and widest Muslims in the world, he liked to point out that Iran already had the atom bomb. "And we could flatten the whole bunch of you." When my dad used to say the Egyptians invented civilization, Ali used to say we invented chess and backgammon.

Then there was Aykut, an Iraqi-Kurd who lived in Offenbach, also a cab driver. I think Aykut was the only one of my father's friends who was worried about him always talking about religion on the taxi stand and not joking about dirty German women and things like before. Aykut was always well-shaven, wore a baseball cap, had a thick, full beard, and chewed gum. He was always wearing an oversize money bag not for cash but for everything he thought he needed to protect his incredibly attractive daughter from the kuffar of Frankfurt: a switch blade, a cutthroat razor, pepper spray, and a piece of metal pipe.

My dad pointed at the flag, saying aggressively, "Your kuffar uncle put you up to it."

"It's just a flag, Farouk, calm down," said Tony the Catholic.

"No!" shouted Ali the Shia. "The US are Satan. In Tehran these flags are burned in the street or used as toilet paper. They are only there to be spat at!"

I noticed that my father was getting more and more uptight. "Tarek, how many times have I told you what these devils do in the world. They kill all the Muslims and do politics with the Jews against the Arabs. That piece of toilet paper isn't coming into this house! What would Sheikh Hamed say when he comes around? What would the brothers in the mosque be saying?"

"Yeah, but Farouk, your brother lives in the States, doesn't he?" said Aykut, laughing and chewing his gum.

My father was about to go ballistic because Aykut was right. My uncle Mohammed had been running a bagel shop in NYC for years, and my father had in former times toyed with the idea of joining in. It always made him wild that his brother was earning more with Jewish bread rolls than he was driving in Germany.

He turned on Aykut, threatening, "You want insult me like that in front of my son?"

"Farouk, stay cool, it's just a piece of rag," said Aykut.

"Piece of rag?" roared my father. "You Kurds have no honor. Someone promises you a piece of a cabbage field for Kurdistan and you do anything for them."

I noticed Ali watching Aykut like a cat. I knew that Ali hated Kurds.

Then, Aykut said poisonously, "You know what I do when I meet an American or an Englishman? I shake their hand for what they have done for us."

Ali and my father laughed derisively. "You thank the devil? What are you for a fool?" asked Ali.

Aykut stood up, saying, "I thank them because they saved us Kurds from Saddam Hussein, who poison-gassed 5000 of us at Halabdscha."

"Aykut," said my father, pointing across at him. "Saddam Hussein was a great and good man. He lowered illiteracy in Iraq and build roads."

Ali sprung into the air. "Are you all insane? He attacked Iran. He attacked the Shia and we defeated him, the dog."

My father leapt to his feet. "He was right to attack you! You filthy sect! Flogging yourselves with chains till your backs bleed. What sort of Islam is that?"

"A sect?" screamed Ali, smashing his fist down the table. "The Shia are the only Muslims, the Sunnis are just a Jewish cult!"

Suddenly, Tony, their token Christian, stood on the sofa, saying, all sermon-like, "Whether Shia or Sunni, it's just all Sushi!"

Nobody laughed. My father walked across to him threateningly. "Don't. Insult. Islam. OK?" Tony got down from the sofa and backed away, a little frightened. "Come on guys, haven't you Muslims got any sense of humor?"

"'Course we have," said Ali.

"That right?" said Tony. "Tell me an Islamic joke then, a really funny one." Nobody spoke.

"No offers?" said Tony. I noticed that he'd backed away by now to the wall on the other side of the room like putting distance between him and them.

"Ok, let me try one. How do you begin a joke about Islam?"

No one spoke.

"You look over your shoulder."

I noticed that my father, Aykut, and Ali were deliberately looking at their shoes. Ali broke the silence. Looking up, he said, "You Christians are worthless trash, you laugh when somebody insults your religion. No honor at all!"

"Honor, honor, honor," mimicked Tony. "Honor, honor, honor… that's your excuse to start killing people about nothing. If the Israelis didn't have you by the throat you would have murdered all the Jews and the Christians in the Middle East long ago. You pack of Jihadists."

Now my father really lost it and began waving his arms in the air and screaming at Tony: "What about the Crusades? That was your Jesus lunatic. Killing all the Muslims and talking about forgiveness and brotherly love…you Christians want to turn the other cheek and we Muslims'll chop your heads off."

"Allahu Akbar," bellowed Ali and Aykut, together punching the air. My mother and the other women suddenly appeared from the kitchen, startled by the shouting. "Everything OK here?" asked my mother.

"This is a matter among men, all women back to the kitchen," replied my father. The other women obeyed immediately. My mother hesitated for a moment, then shook her head and followed them.

"Now you're showing your true colors, aren't you?" said Tony teasingly. "24/7 Jihad in Frankfurt and all women back to the kitchen. Well done!"

My father simply shook his head.

"Say what you like, we still have the bomb," says Ali.

"Great," answered Tony. "What you gonna do with it? Bomb Rome and Jerusalem at Christmas?"

"Wait and see," said Ali, leaning back and smiling in his chair.

Toni laughed out loud. "And thereby destroying the Al Aqsa mosque, your own holy site, you stupid pack of psychopaths. Thank God there is an Israel!"

"You dare to defend Israel? For me, the Jew is just an animal. Bring me one here and I shoot him on the spot," hissed Ali.

Toni was red in the face and turned to my father, saying, "Farouk, why don't you say something to him? This is your home he's talking in, in front of your own son."

"Because Ali is right," said my father. "Don't mention my son. The Jews are all child murderers. And what they need Toni, you jerk, is what the Hamas and Hisbollah can give them, they deserve nothing else."

Tony stood up, saying, "Where are your heads at? You come here from broken-down countries ruled by mad men and you're living in democracy in Europe and you've got jobs and homes, health insurance and civil rights, and do you say a word of thanks? No! You actually want the people in your host country to be butchered by your filthy religious brothers." Tony slumped down on the floor in the corner, looked up at the others, and said, slowly and deliberately, "You know something, guys? Jesus and Gandhi and Mother Theresa and Martin Luther King and The Blessed Virgin herself should come down from heaven and collectively spit on you all!"

It occurred to me afterwards that during the course of this whole conversation I'd been standing there, sort of symbolically holding the American flag. My own little Alamo. But my dad wasn't the type of guy to forgive or to forget because the very next evening he came storming into my room, grabbed the Stars and Stripes, which was hanging out of my window, and slapped me across the face, saying, as he walked away, "This rag is going where it belongs, into the trash can of history." I guess I surrendered the flag.

The Gauland Twins

Would you like to know where hate comes from?
"Eat! You sand nigga swine," yelled Mathias, pushing my head towards the dog turd that lay on the ground beneath me. His twin brother, Andi, was holding me at the same time in a half-nelson so that I couldn't escape. Mathias and Andi, who everybody called the Gauland Twins, really loved to bully and torture me like they did to all the other kids in the neighborhood. Today it was my turn again. We were on the soccer field near my school. Today I got lucky because an old lady came by and broke it all up. Everybody in the neighborhood knew that the Gauland family were neo-Nazis, and they didn't care if anybody knew it. My parents always told me to stay away from them. I'd known them since kindergarten, and we often built sandcastles together until we were all about five years of age, when they realized that I wasn't Aryan enough to be allowed to exist in their world. By the time we were nine years old, their mother, Frauke, who used to beat them black and blue in her drunken fits, had managed to make two fine, upstanding little Waffen SS elite soldiers out of them, to her enormous pride. As a substitute for their unknown father they had had an endless series of thug-like, romper-stomper skinhead boyfriends of their mother as positive

male role models. They used to roam around the streets of Bockenheim with their shaved heads, Doc Martin boots, and Londsdale jackets, accompanied by their household pet, a Staffordshire Pitbull Terrier. They loved to play openly with their butterfly knifes and there were rumors that they were given to murdering cats—a rumor that they never made any effort to deny. Even before their voices had properly broken, they were a passable copy of the skinhead legends of our city. Because I was a loner and looked like an Arab, I was their perfect victim. They robbed me at knife point, half drowned me in the swimming pool, set their pitbull on me, threw me in a construction hole, and tried to stone me to death. "You're used to this, Tarek, where you come from." And they generally kicked and beat me whenever we met from one end of the street to the other. Out of shame I never told my parents about this. My mother would have probably told me to forgive them, but my father would have despised me as a coward and a disgrace to Arabs, Islam, and the Umma.

One day I was hanging out on the football field, and with a sinking feeling in my stomach, I saw the Gauland Twins walking towards me. It was too late to run.

"Tarek, you camel jockey," said Mattias, as they came up to me. Trying to be as friendly as I could, like I was happy to see them: "Hi Andi, Hi Mattias! Great that you're here, wanna practice penalty shooting?" I asked.

"Do you know who Hitler was?" asked Mattias.

"No."

"He did the world a favor, Tarek."

"Yeah?"

"He gassed all the Jews." His brother Andi grabbed the soccer ball I was holding out of my hands, and turning his back to me, kicked it as far away as he could. Then the both of them stood as close to me as they could, staring and grinning into my face. "Hey," I said, "did you watch the match yesterday? Good, wasn't it?" hoping against hope that the inevitable beating wouldn't happen.

"No," said Mattias. "We were visiting our grandpa in Bornheim."

"He," said Andi, "is a proper German, an Aryan, and not an Arab scumbag like yours."

"Or a goat herder like your dad," said Mattias. The Gauland Clan were all very proud of this grandfather of theirs, who they said had served in the Waffen-SS in the Nazi times and had a lampshade made of human Jewish skin, a souvenir of his service at a concentration camp in Poland.

"Hey Tarek," said Andi, "did you know that our grandfather's sister died in Auschwitz?"

"Oh, I am sorry," I said.

"Yeah," said Mattias, "she fell off a control tower." And the pair of them started laughing, the whole time fixing me with poisonous looks.

"And did you know," said Andi, "that at the opening ceremony of the Olympics in Berlin, Hitler thanked the Jews for providing the ashes for the running track." Both of them doubled up again with laughter. I realized that they were just parroting the racist jokes they were hearing at home from their mother and her boyfriends.

"How long, Tarek, does it take an Arab woman to crap?" asked Andi.

"Nine months!" yelled Mattias, right into my ear.

I backed away from them, saying, "Listen guys, leave me alone, OK?"

Andi grabbed me by the throat: "You got a problem with us, camel boy?" Then Mattias, from behind, hissed in my ear: "Sand nigga, you gotta understand one thing: We are German, we are tribal German, and you are just the dirt on our shoes."

Without warning, Andi headbutted me full in the face and a split second later his brother smashed his fist into the side of my head. I was lying on the floor stunned when they both began to lay into me with their Doc Martin boots, kicking me all over my body, shouting the whole time like mad men: "Sieg Heil! Sieg Heil! Sieg Heil!" After what seemed like forever, they stopped and I curled up on the floor like a fetus, crying.

"Next time, we'll gas you, Tarek, you filthy subhuman." Then they both opened the zips on their jeans and urinated on me head to foot, walking away laughing like it was the most normal thing in the world. As the left the field I saw through blurred eyes a stray dog walking towards them. They stopped and saluted it with outstretched arms yelling: "Heil Hitler!"

I lied on the floor for a long time, I don't know how long, in the dirt and in the urine and the pain. Nobody came by. Since that time, I have had tinnitus, a ringing and buzzing in my left ear, and a deep, angry, incurable hatred in my being that would one day find its terrible outlet. INSHALLAH!

Why I like Jews

From the very first day when he saw the camera of his father, David Fleischmann, an eleven-year-old Jewish boy from Bockenheim, knew what he was going to be: The greatest fashion photographer the world had ever seen. He lost all interest in football and swimming and only had eyes for the fashion world of Paris, London, and New York, because he knew already at the age of eleven that life was too short for childish things and that every day counted if he was to achieve his goal of surpassing losers like Helmut Newton and David Bailey and leaving them far behind.

David had long curly hair, red cheeks, and was much too fat for his age. Upon discovering fashion photography as his true calling, it was as if he was born again. He began plundering second-hand shops in Frankfurt, buying with his limited pocket money what he saw as the proper clothing for a man in his line of work. He would appear in an old fur coat or an English tweed suit with a Panama hat on his head, a big plastic ring on his finger, and a walking cane in his hand, and smelling like he'd bathed in aftershave. One day I met him walking to school along Leipzigerstraße.

"Hey Tarek," he cried. "Just look at me! I'm already a made man! The secret of life is if you wanna make it big, then dress British and think Jiddish!"

This all didn't make much sense to me because I have known him all my life (and his family too), and I knew that the Fleischmanns, who also lived in a cheap apartment in the Falkstraße, were as modestly situated as my own family—not poor, but just ordinary working people. But I came to realize that David was completely convinced that if he dressed and acted like a great fashion photographer, that's what he would become, a sort of self-fulfilling prophecy and I began to envy him. When I, with my inferiority complex and ADHD disorder, saw this little, fat, loud-mouthed Jewish kid with his incredible selfconfidence, optimism, and what the Jewish folks call "Chuzpe," I was fascinated by him and began spending more and more time with him in and out of school. I just felt good in his company and it was great to be with him, seeing him jumping around like a madman on the streets, photographing everything that moved with a plastic camera that had no film in it. His dad was a cab driver like mine; they even knew each other and used to talk and argue about the six-day war and stuff like that on the taxi stands.

His mom worked at the checkout at the Woolworths on the Leipzigerstraße. On account of him telling everybody who would listen, soon the whole neighborhood knew about David's obsession and plans.

One day he grabbed hold of me after math class, full of excitement, and said, "What are you doing later, Tarek?"

"Homework, I think."

David waved his ringed finger dismissively, saying: "Forget it, Tarek! There are bigger things in life than mere homework…I need your help this evening. I need you on the spot!"

"What are you up to?" I asked.

"My first photoshoot. It's gonna be pheee-eee-nomenal! And you're gonna be there too." As he was telling me this, his whole face was radiating with energy and he was jumping from foot to foot. I can't remember at all what he was saying but he kept using weird words like "passion" and "muse" and "art."

"It's my first shoot, Tarek, and you're gonna be a model. I managed to get Tina on board, too. She is a great natural talent, the camera is gonna love her."

I knew the Tina he was talking about. She lived across the road from us and was also in our class. I would never have thought of her as a photography model myself, just as the girl with well-brushed hair and an old Raleigh bicycle, but that David must know where undiscovered talent hides. Of course it was impossible for me to say no, David had become a force of nature, and at exactly three o'clock exactly the same afternoon, Tina and I turned up at David's studio. Naturally, what David called his studio was really his bedroom in his parents' apartment, which he intended to use for his art.

He greeted us as we arrived with wide-open arms, shouting joyfully: "Darlings! Loves! Dears! How lovely, how wonderful that you are here! Tina, you look celestial! Tarek, my God, you look so strong, so masterful, so Rudolph-Valentino-like! Believe me, darlings, this is going to be great!"

Then, he confided to us that his name was no longer David Fleischmann; in the future, his name as an artist would be "David Rosenberg." Because Fleischmann was a good name for a kosher butcher, maybe, but not for an international celebrity fashion photography star. As we entered the apartment I instinctively began to take off my shoes.

"No, Tarek!" said David, "Please don't do that. Should I photograph you next to Tina in your tennis socks? Darling, that would be a disaster, an absolute faux pas. Enter my kingdom!"

As we entered the room he announced: "Today, you will witness the incredible beginning of the astounding career of that world-class photographic genius, Mr. David Rosenberg."

I had been in his bedroom before, but I didn't recognize it now. He cleared out all his old things and filled it with a strange collection of objects he obviously found on the street: an old ragged sofa, plant pots with plastic flowers in them, a couple of large broken mirrors, and five very large roadwork signs.

Completing the effect were several old carpets that he hung on the walls. "OK," he said, all business. "First, we do a photo briefing; this is normal in my branch. Sit down!" he exclaimed, pointing at the sofa. We did. Although we only understood a quarter of what this was all about, it was already quite clear to me and Tina that we would be doing everything Mr. Rosenberg told us. And he began with a clap of his hands: "Tina, first we are going to shoot a series with you alone, this is something I have especially thought out for you. The theme of the shoot: the roaring twenties…DADA… Marlene Dietrich…that's your solo number, Tina! And then, Tarek, you come in. You have to see yourself as a type of Latin lover, a young

Don Juan. And Tina, you react cold and rejecting like a Diva, you understand? What I will be capturing on film is an existential human ritual. So show emotions! I wanna see real emotions!" He thought for a moment. "We didn't talk about your fees yet," he said, rubbing his thumb on his index finger. "Don't worry, Brigit Bardot, Kate Moss, Claudia Schiffer…they all have their price. So do you—we talk about it later. This is normal in the branch, OK?"
Suddenly, he walked across the room, lifted up the mattress on his bed, and produced with a manic grin his father's treasured Leica camera, and I thought for the first time on seeing it that this whole thing might end badly.

"Let the shooting begin! I want you to remember that for an artist like me you're just bodies! Bodies, bodies, bodies, nothing but senseless, empty bodies waiting to be given meaning through my photographic lens. You get 20 marks each for the session… you're beginners. This is normal in the branch."

He went across to a shelf in the corner and out of a drawer pulled a small plastic bag and a red tin money box and placed them in front of us on the table. From the money box he took a handful of coins and counted out two piles of 20 marks for each of us. The box looked empty now; it looked like his life savings. He handed Tina the plastic bag. It was full of odds and ends of makeup, lipstick, and stuff which he, I guessed, had stolen from his mother.

"Make yourself up for the camera, Tina, while I sort out some clothes."

While Tina lazily began smearing the stuff on her face, David began sorting through a random pile of women's clothes he had looted from his mother's wardrobe on the floor. Picking up one after another and throwing them down while saying, "Too trashy… too sluttish…too shiksa…too big…too big…oh my God, they're all too big," David seemed to realize there was a flaw in his plan, these being all a grown woman's clothes. He walked across the window and looked out onto Falkstraße for a moment. "They're all too big…too big…" and then, inspired, turned around, saying decisively, "OK! Change of plan…we do the shoot in underwear. An underwear shoot…Tina, Tarek, you're gonna be great."

"No way!" Tina protested.

"I am not dancing around in my johns for you, David!" I said.
We both stood up as if to leave.

"It's Mr. Rosenberg, Tarek, Mr. Rosenberg. And you're both behaving really unprofessionally…or are you? It's just a question of fee, isn't it?" He placed himself between us and the door.

"OK, there are bigger things in life than bar mitzvah!" He crossed the room, climbed up on a chair, and from a shelf took down another box, which I realized was the bar mitzvah box with the money he received now and then from his auntie and uncle from Israel and other family friends for his bar mitzvah in a couple of years' time.

"David," I said, "you're crazy. That's for your bar mitzvah, your family'll kill you." "Tarek, like I said, there are bigger things in life than bar mitzvah." He emptied the whole contents of the box onto the table in front of us. It must have been about 100 marks. I'd never seen so much money before in my life. I guess neither had Tina.

"OK," she said, "let's do it!"

David's face lit up in a big smile. He grabbed his father's camera, turned on his cassette recorder, and the whole room filled up with music from the Village People. For the next 20 minutes, David jumped around taking photos of us like a madman, shouting things like,

"That's great, Tina…you've got it, Tarek…flaunt it, baby, flaunt it!"

I had to hand it to David. He really started to convince me as a photographer, and I began to think that maybe he did have a great career in front of him and really was a natural talent and genius like he claimed. When the session was over, me and Tina, selfish little brats that we were, took his money and went on home. A couple days later, David, still as high as a kite, turned up on the school yard, took me and Tina to one side, and gave us each a signed copy of a photo of ourselves in our underwear by him as David Rosenberg. "You're both just great. By way of thanks here are two mementos from the shoot. Guard them well, they are going to be worth a fortune soon." I took mine home and instinctively hid it well but Tina seemed to have left hers lying around because the very next evening it all hit the fan. Tina's mom saw the photo and freaked right out, thinking that some dirty old man, some drunk from the liquor kiosk at the end of our street, had done something disgusting with her daughter. Tina, in tears, told her mom the whole story about me and David, the camera, the money, everything. And still not really believing her, the whole of her family came over to our apartment. I had a sinking feeling even before I heard the doorbell ring that evening. My mother listened in silence as Tina's parents explained why they were there and she asked me, "Tarek, is this true?" and I confirmed what had happened. Soon, we (Tina, myself, both our moms, and Tina's dad) were all standing outside the Fleischmanns apartment to witness the downfall of the great Mr. David Rosenberg. They found the fiend in his bedroom with a big stack of envelopes containing his photos stamped and addressed to all the leading photo agencies in the world.

The upshot of it was Tina and I had to give the money back on the spot and the Fleischmanns almost killed him for having stolen his father's camera, paying us with his bar mitzvah savings and causing everybody such a lot of fright and distress. As we walked back home along the street I could already hear the poor guy howling. As we got home my father was there after finishing his shift, and my mother told him the whole story. As usual, he went into an anti-Jewish overdrive: "What did I tell you, Tarek, about them Jews? They corrupt, they lie, they steal, they would sell their own grandmothers for money, although they're swimming in it already, and this Fleischmann friend of yours uses his bar mitzvah money to finance his pornographic filt at the age of eleven. How disgusting! Nothing is for the Yahudi sacred, just greed and power and manipulating goyim like he manipulated a fool like you. The half of Frankfurt belongs to them: the banks, the fur shops, half the Kaiserstraße, and the bars and brothels. From this I hope you learned at last, Tarek, like it says in the Quran—that a good Muslim stays away from Jews!"

The next time I saw David was on the following Monday morning in the school yard. I went across to him to say how sorry I was about how things had worked out and how me and Tina had sort of betrayed him. But David just smiled a big broad grin and said, "Listen, Tarek, there is no such thing as bad publicity. It was great PR and what's more it's the role of an artist to provoke a response. Mustn't always be praise—it can be anger, hate, outrage too. If I can manage with my first photos to get the whole neighborhood here in Bockenheim up in arms against me, your family, Tina's family, my family. My mom and dad, they beat me black and blue, and my uncle Moritz from Hanau came by and joined in too. Kicked me on the floor. If I can provoke such a reaction now, then tomorrow Frankfurt, day after the whole country, and one day the whole world is going to be talking about me and my work. It will be gigantic, it will be pheee-nomenal, enormous. Tarek, I am going to be a mega star, just wait and watch me soar! Because I am the great Mr. David Rosenberg, the greatest photographer the world ever saw!"

I didn't know then that that would be one of the last times that I would see him. A couple of days later David and his whole family seemed to disappear from the earth. He no longer showed up at school and when I went round to his house the family was no longer there, a new name was on the door, and the neighbors couldn't tell me where they'd gone. My dad told me that David's father no longer showed up for work. I couldn't understand how an entire Jewish family could suddenly just disappear like that. And I never heard of him again. I find it strange that such a force of nature and ambition could be swallowed up by the universe like that. But I never forgot him, really. To this day sometimes when I am walking along the road or sitting in a streetcar, I'd think of the great Mr. Rosenberg and his legendary shooting session, and I start to smile and then I start to laugh, and I don't care what people around me think. I laugh until I cry.

Just Before The 11th of September

The View from Paul and Heather

In the early spring of 2001 when I was 17 years old, I began a high school exchange year in the small town of Shackleton, Georgia, USA, at the Robert Falcon Scott High School. I lived with the Baptist host family, the Millers (i.e., Heather and Paul) in their house on the corner of Mallory and Irvine Street in a typical southern clapboard house. Actually, I lied to the Millers right from the start. I didn't tell them that my mother was Catholic and my father a Muslim, but in order to increase my chances to get accepted as a guest student, I claimed on the form that I was a Protestant Christian because all I wanted to do was to spend a fun year in America. It worked, and before I knew, I was on the plane, truly excited that at last I was going to the land of my dreams, of Baywatch and Knight Rider and the A-Team, and the land of Louis Armstrong, the first man on the moon. I expected a year of partying and drinking and cruising for chicks in Cadillacs. I didn't realize that I'd be getting pickup trucks, the Baptist faith, and Sunday-go-to-meeting.
After a direct flight from Frankfurt to Atlanta, Georgia, and gor-

ging euphorically on a couple of Double Whoppers and a gallon of Coke, I flew on in a propeller plane to Shackleton. There were only about 20 other people on the plane, and I began to realize that my destination must be in the middle of nowhere and not in a booming metropolis with all the fun you see in Hollywood movies, which was the only picture of the USA I had back then. I pressed my nose to the window and looked at the land beneath us: I saw brought fields growing stuff and little clusters of houses. As I got out of the plane I felt the Georgia heat.

"Hi, you Tarek?" asked a big, strong, broad-shouldered farmer type of guy in a baseball cap, whose clear blue eyes sized me up as he gave me his hand.

"Are you Mr. Paul Miller, sir?" I asked.

"Yep, call me Paul, Tarek! This here is my good wife Heather."

Paul was in his late 30s and had a very strong handshake. He'd been a marine and he looked like one. His wife was a little younger. A good-looking woman with straw-blond hair that she wore tied back tightly. They both had big, friendly grins on their faces. Heather said, "Tarek, we are the Millers, your host family, and we are delighted to have you with us." I noticed that they both had very strong drawling southern accents.

Paul picked up my bags despite my protests, and we all walked across to their grey Ford 15 pickup truck and drove off towards their home. For the first time I was able to see the area where I would spent the next year. We drove past enormous corn and cotton fields, which reminded of the sea. We drove along many-laned highways with huge billboards on either side and lots of wacky little churches completely different from the stone buildings I was used to. And everywhere on the churches, schools, and kindergartens there were signs saying things like "Jesus is alive," "Jesus loves you," and "The Lord is your Savior." I was beginning to realize what they meant by the Bible Belt. I wanted to make as good an impression as possible, so I chatted the whole time, nice and polite to the best of my broken English. Not only was Paul going to be my host father but was also a history and gym teacher at my high school, and with 220 pounds of muscle, he didn't look like the type of guy you could mess around with.

But as we arrived in the Miller's neighborhood, I saw the one-story houses that looked like they were made of card board and the well-mown lawns and clipped hedges, all nice and neat and trim. Maybe it was the heat or maybe the orderliness, but as we walked in to the house I started to get a suffocating kind of feeling that I maybe had come to the wrong place. And this for an entire year, pretending to be a Christian?

Paul put my bags down in the hallway. Heather opened the living room door and a big German boxer dog came out bounding towards me, barking, and Paul said, "Rommel! Sit!" And I thought, *Rommel? They can't mean...*

On that evening, Paul, Heather, and I had our first dinner together: potatoes and gravy and fried chicken. There was a flag on the wall in the kitchen behind me, and I asked Paul what it was.

"That's the flag of the Confederacy, Tarek, good old Dixie," said Paul. And I'm thinking, isn't that the flag of the Ku Klux Klan and slavery that killed Martin Luther King?

"Isn't it a bit racist?" I asked with an embarrassed laugh.

"Nothing wrong with being proud of your country. Part of your past," said Heather seriously.

"Don't you have a swastika someplace in your home back in Germany, Tarek?" asked Paul. I started to think: What kind of conversation is this? What sort of Bible Belt redneck hole have I landed in? They can't be serious.

"No way," I said. "Hitler killed millions of Jews, you must know that." And Paul answered, "really, I don't understand you Germans. Maybe Ay-dolf didn't get everything right all of the time, but the guy is part of your history for heaven's sake. He stood up and fought for his people, so why shouldn't you be proud of the past of your country?" He took a big swig of his ice tea. Because of my social democratic upbringing and all that had been taught to me by my mom and my school in Germany about the horrors of the Nazi past and the remorse we should feel, it was a real shock to me to be hearing my host parents talking like this, like a couple of morons. Maybe they had German roots? Is that why they call their dog after a Second World War German general? Rommel, the brown boxer, was sitting next to me all the time, watching me all the time, hoping to get a chunk from me to eat.

"But he killed all the Jews," I insisted.

"They killed Jesus Christ, Tarek," said Paul.

"Amen," said Heather.

Suddenly angry, I said, "You'll be telling me next that they control the banks and the government as well, like my dad says back home."

"Wow, calm down fella" said Paul. "I guess we're gonna have some real great talks, humdinger, you and I."

"Actually," said Heather, "we wanted to talk to you about the house rules you gotta observe while you're with us, Tarek."

"Yes," said Paul. "This is a God-fearing home and a God-fearing community, as I am sure you are aware. That's why you are here."

"So, Tarek," said Heather, pouring me a glass of iced tea. "We would like it if you only watch television in our company, programs that Paul and I would watch ourselves. That means no MTV or things like that with the girls in bikinis. No cursing or foul language, and we would prefer it if you did not bring young women home. In fact, it would be much easier all around if you maintained a distanced relationship to the opposite sex during your stay with us. No alcohol, no smoking, and certainly no drugs, and we expect you to be home each evening by 9 o'clock at the latest. Any friends you make must be approved of by us."

"You obey these simple rules, Tarek, and we all get along just fine," said Paul.

For me this sounded like the end of the world. At home in Germany I had all the freedom, more or less, of any young kid my age, and here it looked like I was going to have to live like some kind of monk in a monastery. This was a completely different world.

But actually the Millers were really quite nice, I thought. They welcomed me into their life, real friendly and all. They maybe had a few strange ideas, but I felt that they meant well by it. Maybe it would all work out. I kind of liked them.

Later, a family friend of the Millers, Mr. Walker, who was also a teacher at the Robert Scott High school and a colleague of Paul's, came around, probably to have a look at me. We all sat on the sofa watching television. There was a documentary playing about the O.J. Simpson case and Mr. Walker said, "No doubt about it that nigga killed his wife." I looked across at him, unable to believe that this man was a teacher in a school. "But what can you expect," he went on, "the way the world is going, all these faggot boy bands you see yelling and springing around, what sort of influence are they exerting? No wonder a decent football player freaks out and butchers his wife?"

"What does homosexuality got to do with it, sir?" I asked.

"Listen boy," said Paul, "it's like this…if God wanted people homosexual, he would've made Adam and Steve, not Adam and Eve!"

"Amen," said Heather. I really started to feel that I was a long, long way from home.

Robert Falcon Scott High School

Paul was my history and gym teacher at my new school for a year the Robert Falcon Scott High School, Shackleton, Georgia. Right from the start he wanted me to be interested in the football team. In the last season they hadn't won a single game and I think he hoped for some sort of Germanic superman match-winning contribution from me. This didn't work out, not least because I could never work out the rules of the game or what I was supposed to be doing with this egg-shaped ball. Paul didn't seem to mind much really, and I came to realize that in this and in other things he and Heather just accepted that their guest student, Tarek, was different in many ways. It didn't seem to worry them much that I couldn't play football and had some strange ideas.

A typical school day began at 6:30 with Heather turning the lights on in my bedroom, and I'd go downstairs and there would be cereal and orange juice on the table. Paul would already be there reading the local newspaper and eating Fruit Loops with milk out of a big Atlanta Falcons bowl with a huge cup of coffee. He never talked much in the mornings; he'd just say "Morning, Tarek," and get back to his reading. Heather used to run around making sure that I had all the stuff I needed for the school day and when breakfast was finished, I'd drive with Paul in his pickup to school. I'd sit in the passenger seat with my school bag on my lap as Paul drove with a coffee cup in one hand. Every morning was the same ritual of Paul running through this and that, about what was going in school that day, as I looked out the window at the sun rising over Shackleton and the morning traffic, only half listening to what he was saying.

A normal day at Scott High was like I imagine it is at every American high school. Every morning before class there was the Pledge of Allegiance, where you put your hand on your breast and swear to

something or other. Then there was class till noon, then lunch, and in the afternoon there was football training— each day, everyday.
Like every new pupil, I was introduced to the class, and they asked me what they probably asked every new German: if Adolf Hitler was still alive and if we have internet yet. Near to school was also the Miller's Baptist church where they worshipped every Sunday. It was always packed full, and of course I always had to be there too. The first couple of times it was interesting because it was new, but after that, it just bored me to death. But I still had to be there. Some of the other guys from school who I saw there used to take notes with pencils in little books they brought with them, of everything that the minister, a guy called Reverend Riley, used to say in his sermon. Because I was sitting there between Heather and Paul, I had to start doing this myself so that I wouldn't look out of place.
Always not far away was the only other German exchange pupil apart from me: an absolute geek named Martin from somewhere in Bavaria who managed to combine German efficiency and Baptist piety to such an extent that I was afraid he was practicing for another Waco or Guyana. I used to see him sitting there, pressing his hands together as though in a fever, with his head bowed down and babbling something like "Lordy, Lordy" the whole time. I just couldn't bring myself to go that far.

"Lordy, Lordy, oh my Lordy." Not me. No way!

The Age of Dissent

Time went by and the whole integration thing, getting along with everybody in my new community proved to be harder than I thought it would be. For some reason I didn't really like my southern state Dixieland friends all that much. Maybe I'd never gotten over my initial culture shock or I just couldn't get my head around their conservative religious worldview. They got on my nerves when I'd mentioned my heroes like Nelson Mandela, Martin Luther

King, or Rosa Parks, who my mom had told me about in glowing terms. But here, you mention their names and they'd say, "Yeah he/she was OK, but…" and basically conclude that they were fakes and frauds in reality. I suspected because they were black. I guess I was born with an arguing gene in me. A contradiction gene. Something I inherited, maybe…just look at my father in Frankfurt. Shouting in the streets about Jews. And here in Shackleton I thought I could still sense some of the old Confederacy slave and racism culture coupled with Stone Age Darwin-bashing; they believed the earth was 6000 years old, for heaven's sake. It was down to me to give them the enlightened European modernday scientific man of progress in overdrive, both barrels full. For example, in class I would use every occasion I could for whatever reason—whether it was relevant or not—to ram the Theory of Evolution down their throats; or in Bible class, when the homo-bashing, racist minister Riley would be making a point, I would throw in with a passionate defense of gay black pride. Good, healthy adolescent dissent. Whether I understood it or believed it or not. Boom Boom! It just felt so good! And everybody started getting uptight about me—the teachers, the pupils, all of them—and regarded me to be this Arab guy from Germany, a real, fresh, loud-mouthed punk who liked to give it large and thought he was the smartest guy around. I ended up arguing with almost everyone who thought they knew better than me, and this of course didn't gain me any friends. Day by day, I became an outcast loner-type who no one wanted to spend time with. This all happened real quickly.

If you think that a kid at my age would feel bad about that, you're wrong. I really enjoyed the situation. I reveled in it. I was at the high point of my adolescent ego trip. Paul tried his best to find me a couple of friends, but that didn't work out either. I was too far gone. I was looking down from a very high pinnacle at the folks of Shackleton and seeing just a pack of retard, redneck, stone-age, dumbeddown hillbilly boondock hicks. So there I was, lonely and isolated and more than a little homesick. Then, the feeling that somehow I'd been tricked because I wasn't in the America of Tupac, Michael Jordan, and Mike Tyson, but in this boring, religious, conservative prison society.

What made everything worse was that I'd gotten a crush on this really beautiful girl named Nancy, who was a real high school prom-queen type and way out of my league. I tried asking her out for a date and she, well, basically just laughed in my face. What made it worse was that her boyfriend Jason was this really loathsome sport jock, as it turned out, the absolute hero of the high school football team. The perfect alpha male. Everybody was laughing at me, the Kraut Arab jerk. Like I'd been messing with the massa's woman. I just crawled away for a couple of days, wanting to die.

But after a while, embarrassment seemed to turn into anger and a need to strike back. Somehow, slowly but surely, I worked out a plan in the watches of the night. I'd show the people of Shackleton something that they had never seen before. Let's see how they're gonna deal with this one, I thought. I would shake them out of their smug little world alright. Just wait and see! In a way, I was born for the role.

Islam Act

"What do you mean you wanna be Muslim?" exploded Paul, almost falling of the sofa.

"It's been growing within me for some time," I replied.

"But yesterday you were a Christian," said Paul, looking at me in disbelief. "I mean, you went to bed last night a Christian, and you wake up in the morning a Muslim. How does that work?"

"I guess Allah moves in mysterious ways, Paul. It's how it is, you know." It was Sunday morning, and like every Sunday morning, the

Millers were getting ready to go to church and me along with them. Today, it was gonna be different.

"Hey, Heather!" shouted Paul into the kitchen, "Can you come in here?"

Heather came in, with a questioning look on her face. "Heather, we have a problem," said Paul.

"A problem?" asked Heather, concerned.

"Yeah…hmm…Tarek just told me that he woke up this morning a Muslim."

"What?" asked Heather, "just like that?" She looked at me, concerned. "Are you OK, Tarek? Are you feeling ill or something? Can I make you an orange juice?"

"Listen" I said, " with coming to church with you… you can forget that, period! I am convinced in my mind that I've found the truth in Islam. I hope you have the greatness of spirit to accept this. You go to your God, but from this moment on, I'll only be praying to Allah and living in accordance with the teaching of his prophet Mohammed, peace be upon him." Paul, who usually appeared so strong and confident, bent forward, placing his head between his hands and saying something like, "This is all we needed."

Heather said quickly, "Look guys, we can talk about this later, 'cause we gonna be late for church. Umm…so you're not coming with us, Tarek?…OK… umm…your breakfast is in the fridge."

I heard their pickup truck moving off. I looked at Rommel, who was lying on the floor watching me, and I said to him, "Jawohl! Mein General Rommel, this is going to be a whole lot of fun."

A couple of days later, we had just finished football training and were all sitting in our sweat-soaked gear on wooden benches in the locker room. As usual, Paul gave us his after-training talk. "Ok guys, great work today, and when Brian is fit next week, we got a good chance of winning the game against Tanglewood. We'll show 'em guys. Just another thing before we break up: John Clifford will be training you on Friday 'cause Heather and I are going to Tampa regarding our adoption plans. Guess you all heard that Heather and me can't have kids, so we just gotta try another way of starting a family, right?" I was astounded that Paul was standing there, telling the whole team in the locker room private stuff that I only heard around the kitchen table. In Germany it would be impossible for a teacher to be telling that kind of stuff to his pupils, but here, the line between private and public seemed to be pretty hazy. Private stuff would be talked about in church, at work, all over the place, as if it was the most normal thing in the world. I guess they felt it made things easier for them not having to walk around with a bunch of dark secrets. But at the same moment, I realized that my entire school and church and the whole town of Shackleton must know already about me becoming a Muslim overnight. A thing like that gets around. It was certain that Paul had told everyone at school, and because this was a really hardcore Baptist place, they must be taking my change of faith pretty seriously. Although no one apart from Paul and Heather had spoken with me about it, when I thought about it, there had been certain signs and I had the feeling that this was the silence before the storm. At home the situation was tense. At lunch, when we'd normally hold hands and pray, saying grace together and thanking the Lord, I no longer took part, and Heather and Paul would hold hands together and I'd just sit there staring at my plate. It was all pretty uncomfortable but all part of the show. Heather passed me the plate with aubergine.

"Tarek, you wanna come with us to Tampa on the weekend? We can visit the alligator farm on the way and we could drop in on Grandpa Clifford as well. You could meet my dad."

Poor old Heather, she was trying really hard. "No, guess I'll stay here, go to the library, and deepen my knowledge of Islam."

Paul looked across the table at me, and for a moment I saw a real flash of anger in his eyes, but he got it under control. I looked down at my hands pretending to be deep, deep in thought, like I was considering my Muslim obligations and duties or something, shouldering the burden, the heavy burden of being the only Muslim in Shackleton. I constantly had to build up this impression that as a good Muslim convert I had to distance myself from the unbelievers. The atmosphere between the three of us was cooling down all the time. Then Paul suggested with a kind of forced heartiness,

"Hey guys, let's all go fishing at the lake this afternoon!"

"Great idea," said Heather, with forced enthusiasm. "Fish'll be biting good."

"It'll be good to have fish on the table this evening. What do you say, Tarek? Catching a fish or two can't be a crime against Islamic law?" said Paul with a winning smile. "Not that I know of, Paul," I had to admit. And so we all went down to the lake. They won that one.

Fundamentalism for Beginners

As the weeks went by I often found it difficult to maintain my role as a Muslim, which is no surprise, seeing as I didn't believe in it myself but was only acting. In a strange way, though, the whole charade helped me a bit with my homesickness because by acting as a Muslim in Shackleton, I felt closer to home in Frankfurt by thinking of all the Muslim loons I knew there and using them for inspiration. Mad Muslims from memory.

I really had to concentrate the whole time so that I didn't let things slip and allow people to think that I wasn't serious about it (my conversion and so forth). What spurred me on was my dislike of the place, which was getting worse and worse because this whole clean, wholesome goody-goody Baptist world was so different from the Hollywood and rap music images I brought with me. The more I got worked up about it all, the easier it was to act like a Muslim radical. I wanted to show them something they haven't seen before. Not just that type of teenage revolt they were used to—hippies, punk rock, heavy death metal goths, or subhuman rapper scum. All that fake, phony defiance by mama's boys. No! I was gonna shock 'em, give them the real thing, the broken end of a Coke bottle: pure, unadulterated, fullfrontal, hardcore. live Jihad! That's what these rednecks needed, to be confronted, I thought, by a fundamentalism dumber and more extreme than their own. And what could provide that better than good old-fashioned Jihad? They say they believe in religious freedom? Then they have to accept me like I am. I decided to orientate myself to the teachings of my old friend and guide, Sheikh Hamed from the Galluswarte. His theology was really simple and easy to follow: All people who ain't Muslim are dirty, unclean things, more worthless than pigs and deserving only death. Praise be to Allah!

I really enjoyed spreading this message around school and on the streets of Shackleton; a whole lot of fun. Real, shocked looks on their faces. I liked to follow this up by talking politely, but making it clear to my conversation partners that in my opinion, and that of 1.5 billion other right-thinking Muslims on this planet, that Islam will conquer the world and that it is folly to oppose it. It wasn't that I was trying to sow some sort of seed of Islam here in Georgia that would nurture and grow. I just wanted to threaten and hurt everything these rednecks believed in: Jesus and church and ball games and their beautiful USA!

The only problem was that I didn't really know much about Islam because after my parents split up when I was about 11, I didn't have much contact to my dad and his Muslim friends. What I did know,

I'd mainly forgotten. For example, how you pray and how often, when you fast, what you eat, who you may or may not talk to, or the correct attitude to dogs and women. All that remained clear in my mind was that whole bunch of crazy stuff I'd been hearing
from the Terror Sheikh and my dad and his taxi friends and Ehup and Muaviz—things about Jews and kuffar and chopping off heads and killing your sister. I thought there must be more to Islam than that. Finding out then about Islam wasn't as easy as it is now, with YouTube documentaries and other resources. I had to start from scratch with my pioneer project, "Self-Islamization in the Bible Belt." So I started to research in books in the public library and on-line in the computer room at Falcon High, and after some intensive study I got it down pat, mastered the basics: pray five times per day, wash yourself before, and make sure that you always eat haram food and never halal. I had deepened my knowledge of Islam.

The halal and haram food stuff was a bit of a nightmare, a little on the complicated side. So, I was happy to find out that Ramadan was coming soon, when I wouldn't have to eat or drink at all for 4 weeks. But all the same, Heather was a great help in all this. When I explained to her that on religious grounds that I couldn't eat a lot of the food she cooked anymore, she reacted really cool and set up a separate ice box for me in the kitchen with halal food in it, actually cooking halal for me extra. It was all a bit hit and miss, but at least I had the feeling that I was conforming to Muslim dietary laws. Paul used to like to tease me at meal times, waving spare ribs and pork sausage and the like at me till Heather told him to leave me alone. Mainly I was eating vegetarian: a lot of yoghurt and cereal and stuff. For some reason I had the idea that chocolate was haram, so I'd even given up on eating that. Sweet, sticky things are just for the kuffar. Heather was worried about me losing weight, but Paul would say with a laugh, "Looks like our Muslim boy is simply wasting away."

Then there was praying, of course: "Salah," it's called. This had to be done five times a day, and I had to wash myself beforehand five times from head to foot. Muslim folks call this "Wuduu." Honestly, this was torture. Five times a day in the Miller's bathtub. My skin started to dry and crinkle up. It was really important to me to show them how sincere I was, so I prayed five times a day at all the right times, including the morning prayer at 4:30 am. Heather and Paul of course were always woken up by the sound of me running the bathtub at 4:00 in the morning. Sometimes Paul would come out of the bedroom and shout, "Are you going completely mad or what?" At the start, I had a little problem with the praying. I didn't know that you had to say the prayer softly. I thought that you had to howl it out as loud as you can like a muezzin in a minaret in Cairo. The first time I prayed at 4.30 in the morning, I was standing freshly washed in my bedroom, on my towel which I used as a prayer mat, and I shouted as loud as I could: "Allah u Akbar!…". Shocked out of their lives, Paul and Heather stormed into the room: "What's wrong? Did something happen?" they asked. "I am making Salah! Worshipping Allah. Get used to it!" I said.

The next day I was doing the evening prayer in my room, kneeling on the floor with the door open so they could see me. Paul and Heather came in, and Paul said "Hey Tarek, I remember reading in National Geographic that you Muslim guys have to pray towards your holy city of Mecca, and Mecca is east of here."

From the floor I looked up at them and asked, "So?"

"Because you're praying to the northwest, Tarek. You are praying towards Alaska," said Paul, grinning.

"You know, Tarek, I don't know much about your prophet Mohammed," said Heather, "but I am pretty sure he was never in Anchorage."

"Boy didn't even make it to Wyoming," said Paul. And they both started laughing. So I twisted around on the floor clockwise a couple of feet and carried on praying, seething with anger. "Now you're praying to New York City, Tarek," said Paul. Barely controlling my anger, I twisted further to the right.

"Warmer, Tarek, Baltimore," said Heather. "You've got to reach Miami, then you got it right." And they both doubled over laughing. I stood up, grabbed my towel, and left the room, shouting,

"Stop laughing at my beliefs! Stop laughing at Islam!" slamming the door behind me. Paul followed me towards the door of the house, saying "Oh, come on, Tarek, me and Heather were just joking around." Blaspheming infidel swine. Burn in hell.

The Miller's Home Library

The next day, I was still upset. It was a usual hot Sunday morning in Georgia, and since I had stopped going to church with the Millers, I was hanging around outside on the street, waiting for them to come out like every boring Sunday. I felt a little conspicuous because at this time of the day on a Sunday the whole of Shackleton is in some House of God, so the streets were empty except for me and a couple of stray dogs. When the service was over, Paul and Heather came out with the rest of the congregation, and after a while, when they all talked and laughed a bit together, me, Paul, and Heather got into the car and drove to the Waffle House. We drove along the highway with its corn fields on both sides and the sun burning down from the sky.

"Look, Tarek, we gotta talk," said Paul.

"Yeah," said Heather, "don't you feel bad about last night, me and Paul were just joking." "But you don't make it easier for us either, hanging around outside the church," said Paul.

"It's kind of embarrassing for us," said Heather.

"It's not that we don't respect your beliefs, but we're getting a lot of negative feedback from all the folks here," said Paul. "It was a given right from the start that you'd come to church with us," said Heather. "We know," said Paul "that you're going through some sort of identity crisis here, but all the same you could at least get it together to join us in church."

Because I didn't want to hear anymore moral preaching from them, I said, "Yeah, like I'm sorry, maybe I'll think about it." We drove on in silence to the Waffle House. As we were eating waffles and syrup and drinking coffee in the middle of the Sunday morning crowd, Paul said "Tarek, I get the feeling you think that we're just some backwards Baptist people here living in the middle of nowhere with no idea of the world. But things are more complicated than that. Not so simple."

And Heather joined in, saying "Like Paul, you know? He served in the army in Iraq. Reserve officer. Desert Storm. Saw a whole lot of really bad stuff."

"And Heather," said Paul, "she was with her Christian volunteer group two years in Mexico City in a real mean slum." And I said, "Yeah, yeah, you were both in Eisenach visiting Martin Luther. That's so typical American. Wars around the world made up for with a bit of dogooding and all around it off with little trip around Europe."

Paul raised his eyebrows and said to his wife, "These are the times that try men's souls."

Back at the Miller's place it was late afternoon, and I sat with Paul on the couch in the living room while Heather was running through the house doing stuff. And then I asked him, "Hey Paul, who was that from? That bit about men's souls you mentioned sounded too good for you."

Paul looked me straight in the eyes: "From Tom Paine." Then he got up and walked across the room to the bookshelves. The Miller's had on their living room wall a shelf full of books that I hadn't paid much attention to before. Must have been about six square feet. He pulled a book out of it, then cameback and sat down next to me. He showed me the
title of the book. It was "The Age of Reason." He began to flick through it, saying, "This here is from him, Tom Paine. I can lend it to you if you'd like. Think you'd find it interesting." I didn't want to show Paul that the quote and the book had awakened my interest, so I said simply, "Yeah, sure," and took it from him. I looked at the cover and said with a low voice, "The Age of Reason… Hey Paul, you mentioned that you were in Iraq, in the war, I mean?"

"Yeah, and Heather's cousin, Frank, as well," Paul replied.

"You know, Paul, I think all these wars you Americans are doing are a crime against humanity. I mean, you kill thousands of innocent people for no reason."

"Tarek, listen. Things aren't that easy. They're more complicated, more than you think. Heather's cousin Frank, for example, he was a pilot in Iraq. Supposed to hit an enemy position. Precision bombing. They gave him the wrong coordinates. Someone messed up. Hit a children's hospital. Something he has to live with. Tarek, things aren't as black and white as you describe it. There are grey shades, and somewhere in between, the real work is hidden… these are the times that try men's souls." I looked at the book that I was still holding in my hand.

"So, who was this Tom Paine?" I asked.

And Paul said, "An extremist for his time. Perhaps for all time. A real troublemaker. But he wasn't driven by teenage tantrums like you, but by conviction. He said his country was the world and his religion to do good. That's the kind of guy he was." I was thinking to myself: "Where did I hear this before?"

Then Paul continued: "He stood shoulder to shoulder with Jefferson and Washington in the Revolution. He was sentenced to hanging in England for writing about human rights and to the guillotine in France for opening his mouth against Robespierre. And here in the US, by way of thanks, we ignored him to death because we didn't like his attitude to religion. Man died a drunk. Five people went to his funeral. They say he did some good but a lot of harm. To me he is a hero…and you know, Tom, was like an old dog who wouldn't lie down when something disturbed him: he'd go for anyone, and I think he would like the idea of some guy turning up in the Bible Belt and preaching Islam, somehow.…without Tom Paine there probably wouldn't be the USA. Don't get me wrong ,Tarek, I don't hold what you believe or say what you believe, but our Founding Fathers laid down the principle that you have the right to say it. Even here in the Deep South we can take contradictory opinions because those guys made it possible. It's also what makes us strong. Freedom doesn't scare us at all."

Paul got up and walked back over to the bookshelf.

"My dad was a big fan of Tom Paine too," continued Paul, "He said they had something in common: they both survived by chance. Tom escaped from England because his boat sailed 10 minutes early, and he missed the guillotine because of an open door. You may not believe it, but Dad didn't take the family Bible with him to the beaches of Normandy in the second world war. Nope. He had this book of Tom with him. This copy is sort of a family bible, you know. Dad said he survived like Tom, by chance, when the bullets flew past him and his comrades, young men, who died right next to him."

"Maybe it was Allah's will?" I said.

"No, he didn't believe in Allah, he believed in reason, the rights of men, and common sense. He always told me that it was common sense that made America great and that brought us to the moon. Me and Heather have always believed that we wouldn't understand our Christian faith if we didn't understand Tom Paine too….You know something, Tarek, if Dad had been hit by a bullet I wouldn't be here, and if dad hadn't gone to Germany, you wouldn't be here."

"Was Tom Paine an atheist, then?" I asked.

"He said he believed in a Supreme Being, but not one that messes in our affairs," Paul said.

For a split second, I thought that there might be a side of America I wasn't getting. Heather came in. "You guys looking at books?" she asked, and went across to the shelf and pulled out a book. "Here's my favorite, Tarek," she said. "Harper Lee, 'To Kill a Mockingbird'. It's about a lawyer who defends a man railroaded on false charges through racism. It's great."

"I think it's on our curriculum," I said.

She pressed the book in my hand. Then they both took Rommel out for a walk and left me sitting there alone in the living room on the sofa, a book in each hand. I got up and started to have a look at the other books on the shelves. The Miller's Home Library. In addition to Tom Paine, there were works by Benjamin Franklin, Ralph Waldo Emerson, David Thoreau, William Godwin, Edmund Burke, John Steinbeck, Ernest Hemingway, George Orwell, Aldous Huxley, Ray Bradbury, Angela Davis, William Faulkner, Thomas Jefferson, Edgar Alan Poe, Marry Wollstonecraft, Jack London, Mark Twain, Charles Dickinson, William Blake, Oscar Wilde, William Wordsworth, Thomas Carlyle, Joseph Conrad, John Stuart Mill, Bertrand Russel, David Hume, Emily Bronte, James Baldwin, Rudyard Kipling, William James, Valerie Solanas, Henry James, George

Jackson, Sylvia Plath, Dorothy Parker, Virgina Woolf, Richard Wright, Flannery O'Connor, Emily Dickinson, Jane Austen, C.S. Lewis, J.R. Tolkien, G.B. Shaw, John Dewey, W.E.B. Dubois, G.K. Chesterton, Erskine Caldwell, Ernest Shackleton, Robert F. Scott, John Reed, T.E. Lawrence………..

Kuffar Literature

The next morning, after a night in which I think I must have had nightmares about the Miller's books, hundreds of thousands of books, I awoke with just one thought in my mind: It was Sheikh Abu Hamed back in Frankfurt, saying to us, "There is only one book, the holy Quran." And in that moment I realized I needed a copy of the Quran as an antidote to all this as quickly as possible. After school I went into the first book store in Shackleton I could find to get myself a copy. Because I needed to have one to read, didn't I? But also to walk around with it so that everybody could see it in my hand and know that I was a man of the Islamic faith, leaving no doubts in their minds. So, there I was, standing in front of the shelf marked "religion," looking for an English copy because I couldn't read a word of Arabic. I knew I'd be missing the beauty of the original language by reading it in a kuffar tongue, but that I should be happy to find any copy at all here in the Bible Belt. I searched through the shelves but could only find kuffar literature about Jesus and bibles, bibles, bibles all over the place. And I am thinking, when Islam takes over the world, these shelves will be full of Qurans and the Hadiths. Al Hamdulliah. It could only be a matter of time before Shackleton and the whole of Georgia would be part of the Caliphate and all my tormentors would be slaves.

"Sir, can I help you?" asked a middle aged man, interrupting my thoughts. "Yes, sir," I answered. "I am looking for a copy of the holy Quran."

"A holy Quran, sir? I am sure we have one. Just gonna ask my supervisor—Betsy!" He called across to a young woman sitting at the cash register on the other side of the store. "This young man here is looking for a copy of the holy Quran." I noticed that all the other customers in the store were looking across at me with interest.

"Then he must look on the shelf 'Religions of the World,'" answered Betsy.
As I stood in front of the gigantic shelf, I was astounded by this enormous offering of books about different religions and beliefs. Talk about religious plurality. There were copies of the Quran in all shapes and sizes: in English, Spanish, and Japanese. There were books on Bahai, Hinduism, Buddhism, Taoism, Animism, Judaism, Witchcraft, Catholicism, Quakerism, Rastafarianism, Astrology, Scientology, Native American religions, Deism, Shinto, Mormonism, Freemasonry, and a whole lot of stuff I hadn't even heard of. It was dizzying and disconcerting. I couldn't believe that these narrow-minded Baptist hicks could tolerate such a vast array of competing beliefs. How could they live with it when it disturbed even me? Did they want to bring people to the verge of confusion and despair with all this contradictory garbage? I grabbed the next best Quran I could find, paid and left the store. Walking home, I was thinking that they must be mad to let such ideas roam freely in their community. In a decent Islamic state they would be banned, burnt, prohibited. It suddenly occurred to me that I hadn't laughed in weeks. It was scary. Something had changed in me. I had somehow tightened up. My Islam act, my Djihad trip that had started off as a prank seemed to be taking control of me. I'd converted myself. After all, I was living it 24 hours a day and it was coloring my view of the world and the people around me. Things were getting darker and darker, narrower and narrower. And it felt good, my little death cult. Somehow.

This Machine Kills Fascists

One day, I was walking along the mall in Shackleton, heading for the Virgin Records store to build up my collection of gangster rap CDs. Gangster rap from Tupac and the guys, about killing homos and women, seemed to be the suitable soundtrack to the Djihadi frame of mind. Then I saw him in front of a store window, this guy playing guitar. On the floor in front of him was an open guitar case with a couple of coins in it. He was a young guy, maybe a couple of years older than me. He was wearing a brown leather jacket and an old Trilby hat and had long, brown hair down to his shoulders. A real charismatic hippie type. I stopped and listened. He was singing a whole bunch of old Sixties stuff—Lennon, Dylan, and so on. And he was really putting out some positive vibes, smiling and laughing and tripping right along. Nobody stopped to listen; they just kept on walking by. Nobody was standing there, but it didn't seem to trouble him much. I started to envy him. I started to compare his situation to mine. There I was, play acting, living this really lonely, desolate Islam lifestyle mainly out of spite, and here, with this guy singing his hippy songs, free as a bird, having the time of his life. This was pretty depressing. Suddenly, he stopped playing, grabbed a handful of coins out of the case, stuffed them in his pocket without counting, stowed his guitar away, and picking it up, looked at me and said, "Hey man, can you gimme a ride downtown? Gotta meet a buddy of mine who'll give me a place to crash."

"You mean in my car?" I asked stupidly. "I don't have one."

"Ok, that's cool," he said, "I guess I'll catch a bus," and started to walk away.

"No, hold on a minute!" I shouted after him, suddenly afraid that this force of nature was going to disappear from my life. "I really like the way you play."

"Yeah?" he asked with a laugh, "You sure? Most guys our age would say that it's moms old hippie music."

"Well, to tell you the truth, back home in Germany my mom's got a whole stack of your kind of thing," I said.

"Really? Your mom was a hippie in Germany? That's great. Sit down." We both sat down, cross-legged like buddhas, in the mall. It felt really good to be sitting next to this guy. I noticed that there were girls walking by and sneaking looks across at us. For weeks, I had been automatically averting my eyes at the sight of women, like a good Muslim should, except with Heather, who'd told me to quit fooling around. But somehow, sitting next to my new found friend, I found myself doing the same as him, staring at their legs as they were walking away.

"You often play here at the mall in Shackleton? Never seen you here before."

"Nope," he said, "today is the first and last time. Just passing through, know what I mean? Everyday someplace else. Just moving along. Just like a rolling stone, no direction home, a complete unknown."

"Where you from?" I asked.

"From a one-horse town, North Carolina way. Heading down to Mississippi. I bum a lift, play a little guitar, and move along, sleeping where I can. I make enough dough playing on the street for eats and coffee and cigarettes."

"Wow," I said, "that sounds really cool. But where are you actually heading to?"

"Clarksdale, Mississippi," he answered.

"Clarksdale, Mississippi?" I asked. "Shouldn't you be going to San Francisco like all the rest?" I said with a laugh.

"No, Clarksdale. That's my destination," he said, suddenly serious.

"Why?" I asked.

"Well, you know man, to tell you the truth, I don't really have that much talent, if you know what I mean, as a musician."

"Sounded alright to me."

"Maybe it did, but you see, man, covering Evergreens in a shopping mall in Shackleton is one thing, but I want more," he said.

"What more could you want?"

"Lemme tell you. I wanna be one of the greatest singer-songwriters of all time. Original stuff. My own unmistakeable voice and sound that inspires people in the future to stand up on their hind legs in nowhere shopping malls, like this one here in Shackleton, and be happy and joyful to cover me! You know what I mean?"

There was something about him that reminded me of my old friend David Rosenberg. Insane ambition maybe.

"And for that reason," he continued, "I am heading down to good old Clarksdale, Mississippi, because that's where the crossroads is, where the great Robert Johnson sold his soul to the devil and became King of the Delta Blues. And I intend to do the same."

"Sell your soul to the devil?" I could scarcely believe my ears.

"That's the price someone like me has to pay, not possessing enough natural talent. You're reduced to doing stuff like that if you wanna be the next Bob Dylan. You can see it as a type of pilgrimage: my pilgrimage to Robert Johnson's crossroads or Dylan's pilgrimage to Woody Guthrie's hospital bed."

"Who was he?" I asked.

"Dust Bowel Refugee…folk singer. He came out of the Great Depression…poverty, hard work…You know John Lennon?"

"He wrote 'Imagine,'" I said.

"Yup, in my opinion, John Lennon was the greatest Limey who ever came to America. 'Cept Tom Paine, of course. What all these guys got in common—Guthrie, Dylan, Lennon—is that they're opposed to fascism, racism, and oppression and for peace, brotherhood, and love."

As he spoke, he looked across at the rap CDs I bought. "Guess we both got different tastes in music. Depends on what you grow up with, I suppose. My folks would be singing Woody Guthrie all the time." He looked across at me thoughtfully. I felt a bit ashamed of this. In order to divert him, I asked about the sticker I'd seen on his guitar, saying, "This machine kills fascists."

"It's what Woody had on his guitar. Yeah, my grandparents were German Jews, got out of there in the 30s just in time…God bless the USA. 'Cept for the limeys, the whole of Europe thought Nazism was the answer to poverty. And what was America's answer?

Social democracy, Roosevelt, and the New Deal. That all come about in my opinion due to guys like Woody, and Tom Paine of course. No way you get around that guy. 'The Rights of Man,' brother, stead of 'Mein Kampf.'"

I could only follow half of what he was saying. He was talking about a world that was strange to me. I just sat there and listened as he talked.

"Yeah man, the music of the Sixties, it all came out of the Sixties. Stuff we take for granted today like Anti-rascism, women's rights, gay rights, ecology. The hippie movement. Flower Power. Haight Ashbury. Woodstock. And they were standing on the shoulders of guys like Tom Paine and his friends. Man, the music of the Sixties, it blew all that marching military stuff away. Joplin, Joni Mitchell, The Doors, Simon and Garfunkel, Dylan, too freakin' much man. The spirit of the Sixties was the spirit of the Founding Fathers. Dylan is the son of Tom Paine. And what did you guys in Germany have at that time? Just a bunch of psycho, political terrorist types like them Bader Meinhoff running around and wasting people. That's a real sad song, man. Only problem is, sad songs ain't selling this year." And then he got up, picked up his guitar case, and slowly walked away without saying goodbye. I watched him walk along the mall until he disappeared, and then I stayed there, sitting alone on the floor for a long time. I realized I hadn't asked him his name. Who cares…just another kuffar.

Don't Tell It on the Mountain

I was becoming more and more isolated. The kids at school had given up talking to me, not wanting to listen to all my Islam sermonizing the whole time. They were actually shunning me, laughing behind my back. As I walked around Shackleton I could sense that the adults also seemed to be looking at me with my Quran in my hand, like I was an unwelcome freak. Therefore, I looked for more and more consolation in Islam. Didn't find much. It was a vicious circle. I didn't even believe in all of this. What had I gotten myself into? Why was I doing this? This was all going nowhere. These people here didn't want to have to deal with me and my problems. The only two people apart from Paul and Heather who seemed to be halfway interested in talking to me were these two black kids at school, Daniel and Christopher. They were the only two African-American pupils at Falcon High, and I thought that must have something to do with it (them being a minority like myself).

Christopher was a big, fat kid weighing about 260 pounds, belly hanging out of his trousers, that sort of thing. Looked like a Sumo wrestler. His sidekick Daniel, on the other hand, was six-feet-five inches tall and as thin as rake. Looked like a Masai warrior. Talk about outsiders. They always hung around together like underdogs do. I assumed that they had been subjected to massive daily doses of redneck racism and discrimination from the moment of their birth. And I thought that with me being an Arab with my thing about Mohammed that we must be natural allies and that they would be more than ready to abandon the ways of the kuffar and embrace the true religion of Islam if I were to explain it to them. So I decided to make Dawah on them. Inshallah.

I spent a couple of days reading Islamic literature in my bedroom until I felt myself ready to approach them with the information that it was Allah who loved them and not Jesus. What made the idea of converting the two of them to Islam even more interesting was the fact that Christopher's father was a minister in the Baptist church here in Shackleton and Daniel's mum was very active in the choir. Since they were here in the white, racist South, with its history of the Ku Klux Klan and lynch mobs, I reckoned that my starting point with them should be with Malcom X and the Black Power Movement, then leading on to the Nation of Islam and perhaps even mentioning the Zebra Killers at a later stage. This would maybe focus and harness their anger against the white racist society around them. I began to fantasize that we three would form the nucleus of a radical Islamic cell, leading to a grassroots movement that would culminate in the Islamization of Georgia and the grounding of a caliphate. Inshallah.

My plan of converting the pair of them to Islam had a twofold purpose. Firstly I wouldn't be so alone anymore, and secondly, I wanted to inflict as much damage as possible upon my environment. I could imagine what kind of shock and outrage the spreading of my Islam infection would produce. If I could convert them, then it would make some sense out of my situation here in Shackleton. Deep down inside, I knew that this whole thing was really just a lot of frustration. My feeling of social constraint here, the monotony of it, the closeness, the church, the football training, the whole day at school, the family meals, the sheer repetitive boredom of it in comparison to my spoiled child-of-divorce lifestyle in Frankfurt. I guess my vanity just wouldn't let me play along.

One Friday evening I managed to get us all together at Christopher's parents' house. It was a big, spooky southern villa-type house, a house with an evil history people said, on the edge of Churchill Park. Me and him and Daniel. His folks were away for the weekend. I waited for a while, waiting for the right moment as we all sat together on the sofa playing some dumb Nintendo game. I planned to convert them in the classic way, by starting off mentioning something interesting about Jesus and then moving on to him being a prophet in Islam and so on: the good old Trojan Horse method. During a pause in the game I felt the moment was right.

"Hey guys, did you know that Jesus is also a prophet in…."

"STOP!" shouted Daniel, standing up and pointing his finger at me.

I looked up at him in surprise. Christopher turned to me on the sofa, saying "Can it, Tarek. We know what your agenda is."

"What agenda?"

"You see, Tarek," said Christopher, "we know that you set this up this evening because you think we are just a couple of young, dumb black kids, religious but ostracized from the white racist society around them."

"And," Daniel went on, "you thought that we would be on account of this ripe for conversion to your Islam faith like so many other black folks have done here in the USA…like rejecting the religion of the Christian slave master. But Tarek, you Muslim Arabs slaved us as well."

"What you don't know, Tarek, but are about to learn, is that you are talking to a couple of atheists and that in America, Tarek, you can have 20 gods or none at all," said Christopher.

"And we decided for none at all, man!" added Daniel.

"Atheists?" I asked, bewildered.

"Yeah," said Daniel, towering over me, "regarding the Black Man, the Christians want him praying on his knees and the Muslims want him praying on his belly. Every which way, except standing up on his hind legs, like a man." Christopher leaned over, crushing me against the arm of the sofa, saying "We ain't Malcolm X, we ain't Farrakhan…you know what?" He pointed at Daniel. "Daniel here is an International Socialist and I am a gay. Yep, a homosexual. And just because I am the son of a preacher man and Daniel the son of a gospel-singing choir lady, you immediately racially stereotyped us."

"A real false assumption," said Daniel.

"How did you guys end up not believing in God?" I asked weakly.

"By intensive reading," replied Christopher.

"We both," said Daniel, "realized that we had a germ of doubt in us about religion, probably because of my political convictions and Chris here's sexual orientation. So we started to read Thomas Jefferson and Tom Paine, for example. The jury's out on those guys, some say they were Deists, some say more than that, like they were atheist…then we read Robert Ingersoll and Bertrand Russel and Marx and Nietzsche and all the atheist literature we could get our hands on. Convinced us totally."

"And that's where we are at," said Christopher, grinning.

"But where did the world come from?"" I asked in confusion, "If there ain't no God?"

"Well," said Daniel, "Chris is inclined to believe that it was always here, but I suspect that it spontaneously created itself out of nothing."

Suddenly the atmosphere got a bit tense and Christopher got up, his enormous body looming over me.

"And if you think, Tarek, that this was easy for us, than you are dead wrong. There was a lot of pain and doubt and self-questioning and fear. Fear of hell and damnation. But we made it through and out the other side."

"And then you come walking through the door, trying to lay another dumb superstition on us," said Daniel, pointing his finger aggressively at me. I stood up and walked away from them, seeking safety in the corner of the room.

"How come your families, the other people here in Shackleton, and the church don't know what you think?"

"Because, Tarek," said Christopher, "We ain't like you. We don't want to hurt our parents, family, and friends by spewing our beliefs all over them. We'll soon be leaving here. We plan to go to college in New York City where we will be able to live our lives openly in all respects, like James Baldwin did. Folks here will get to know it bit by bit without causing too much damage."

And Daniel said, "What he means is 'Don't tell it on the mountain.'"

"What if I tell it, about you guys, I mean?" I asked.

"Then we tie you to a back of a truck and drag you all the way to Franklin," said Christopher.

"Hey guys, I was joking around…I was just talking… it's alright by me, I mean…" I said, "and then after New York and college, what you up to then?"

"OK, Tarek," said Daniel, "you are the first to hear this, strangely enough, but it's maybe appropriate in this situation. We will be studying psychology in NYC and when we get our certificates, we gonna set up our own therapy practice in Manhattan."

"Wow, that's great, guys," I said, thinking, How am I going to get out of here?

"Glad you think so, Tarek," said Christopher. "We got it all thought out, a new type of therapy. You may have heard of Primal Therapy and Gestalt Therapy. Well ours is called Blasphemy Therapy. We'll get the people in a room, sitting on the floor or whatever and have them cursing and swearing against the Gods of their religion all day long in order to free them from the shackles and fetters of religious belief, thereby making them happy, balanced people free of all guilt and neuroses, fears, and obsession."

Then Daniel looked across to Christopher seriously and said, "You know what, Chris? Why we don't make Tarek here our first patient? He has the disease and we got the cure."

Chris nodded in agreement, "OK Tarek, let's go. You repeat after us."

And the two maniacs began a litany of the foulest abuse against my religion imaginable. I had never heard anything like it in my life. They kept urging me to repeat what they were saying. It was the most horrific four-letter filth directed at the icons of belief. They kept yelling at me that I do the same: "Say it Tarek, say it!!! Let it aaall out, Tarek!" They screamed at me: "You will feel better for it!" I panicked, ran for the door, and ran right out of that eldritch house of horror. And the whole time the two mad boys were screaming a demented stream of blasphemy behind me.How badly could a conversion go?

Georgia Lynch Mob

It was round about midnight and I was running through the streets blindly in a state of shock. The evening hadn't worked out like I planned it, preaching Islam, and I was now on the run from a couple of mad black kuffars. I had never heard of anything so sick and insane and I just wanted to get back home. I ran along Wellington and Nelson streets and then lost my way somewhere in Churchill Park, wandering around wondering if I would ever find my way out of here. I was getting really scared because I didn't know where I was and Paul and Heather warned me about all the gangs and crazy people who used to hang out in the park at nights. There were trees everywhere. I could hear some weird birds and insects scratching and screeching around me. On account of this, to build up my courage, I began to shout "Allahu Akbar, Allahu Akbar!" at the top of my lungs to keep the kuffar and wild animals at bay. To my relief, I somehow found myself on a kind of road, and in the distance I saw the headlights of a truck headed towards me. I was saved, I thought. The truck stopped about 30 feet in front of me and the driver and another person got out. They were two really big sized guys and I squinted trying to see them more clearly.

"Hey, look what we got here. Got us the Muslim boy. You looking for your camel, Muslim boy?" said the taller of the two, and I realized to my horror that it was Falcon High's pride and joy, the hero of the football team: blonde blue-eyed Jason. The guy whose girl I'd made a play for and he was now grinning really evilly all over his lantern-jawed face. His friend I knew as well. He was another football jock, A.J., who was built almost as wide as a beer truck and said, "Yeah Jason, looks like it's time for a neck tie party."
"Sure it is," said Jason. "Time we teach this raghead he should just stay away from our women…go fetch the baseball bat, man!"

I turned and ran as fast as I could. Just anywhere. They followed me nice and slowly in the truck the whole time. I just ran and ran and ran, and they were shouting out the window behind me, things like "Run, camel boy, run…we gonna hang you high Muslim boy…you gonna meet your maker…" I was scared that they would run me over with the truck, drive over me back and forth, then finish me off with their baseball bats and hang me from a tree. I was desperately trying to remember what a Muslim says just before he dies in order to get to paradise, but I couldn't. Once again, I was a real disgrace to Islam. My dad would die of shame. And all that time, these two sport jock kuffars were whooping and yelling in their truck behind me: "Die, camel boy, die!" In a panic, I plunged through some bushes to my right and by a miracle I found myself on the corner of Mallory and Irvine Street in front of the Miller's home. I stood still. The truck wasn't there anymore. I sat down on the sidewalk gasping for air, trying to calm down before going into the house. The lights in the living room were still on and I was beginning to feel safe for the first time in what seemed like a long while. And then the truck appeared out of nowhere and screeched to a halt in front of me. In a flash, Jason and his buddy were straight out of the car and Jason picked me up and slammed me onto the hood, holding me down by the throat. His buddy stood next to him holding a baseball bat.

And Jason said, "Now's the time, camel jockey."

"Jason, you wanna tell me what it is you think you're doing?" asked a very calm, steady voice. It was Paul. He was suddenly standing there. He must have heard the commotion and came out of the house. Jason, electrified, let go of me and turned around to Paul. Jason was standing with his arms to his side almost to attention. A.J. did the same. Jason said in a stuttering voice, "G-g-g-g -good evening Mr. Miller, sir! H-h-h-how are you, sir? We just happened to be in the neighborhood, Sir, a-a-and thought that we'd look by."

"With a baseball bat, Jason?" asked Paul "And invite folks to lay on your car hood with your hands on their throat?"

Jason, standing erect with his head sunk to the ground, said, "It's all a great misunderstanding, Mr. Miller, sir. Me and A.J. here, we are just having a bit of a fun with Cam…with Tarek here…nothing serious at all, sir…just horsing around, sir."

"Looked like some pretty serious horsing to me from my window over there" said Paul, pointing towards the house.

"That's because the guy tried messing around with his girl, Mr. Miller, sir," said A.J. helpfully.

"Shut it, A.J.," said Jason, elbowing him. Paul walked right up to the both of them. They looked as if they were just 1 inch tall. And Paul said, "Listen, you two are on my football team. I trained you for years, didn't I? Told you always to leave your egos off the field and respect your opponent? Didn't it occur to either of you muscle-bound morons that those ideas of sporting fair play should also apply to how a man conducts himself in real life? Just because a guy looks sideways at your girl don't mean that you hunt him like a wild animal through the streets of town, slam him on the car, and threaten him with a baseball bat. You wouldn't beat up on the other team just because they scored a goal, would ya? Don't you understand that there are rules in football and there are rules in life, and they're just the same."

And I am thinking, this is Paul doing what he like best apart from football: laying a Sermon on the Mount on someone. Man, did he make me sick.

"You're right, sir, Mr. Miller, sir, you're absolutely right, sir!" said Jason.

"Dunno what came over us, sir," said A.J.

"Won't ever happen again, sir," said Jason.

"This gonna affect our position on the team, sir?" asked A.J., really concerned.

"You gonna suspend us, sir?" echoed Jason. They really looked like a sorry pair. Football was their life, the meaning of their existence. Not that they thought it was religion; it was more important than that.

Paul smiled. "Not if you apologize nice and gentleman-like enough to Tarek here for the unsporting behavior you've showed toward him on this night. Then I guess you'll both get to kick a ball again."

"Like the Queensberry Rules, sir, you mean?" said Jason, sensing hope.

For the first time, Paul smiled. "Yep. That's what I mean, boys."

First Jason and then A.J. came up to me where I was sitting on the side of the car and began apologizing profusely: "I apologize, Tarek, profusely, sincerely, without reservation, nor let or hindrance…"

And then A.J. said, "Yeah, I'm sorry too…like prof… since…let… hind…yeah…like Jason says, I am sorry."

"Listen Tarek, believe us, we are devastated by our conduct, by our abuse of the hospitality of the people of Shackleton to a visitor to these shores, to a person much deserving of better who has been shabbily treated in a shameful manner not in accordance with all we were brought up and taught to believe and we…"

"OK," said Paul, "enough already. No need to overdo things. He gets the message. And he accepts your apology. Don't you, Tarek?"

"Yeah," I said, and shrugged. Paul kept looking at me. I had the feeling that something was expected from me. Didn't know what. We all just hung there for a couple of seconds saying and doing nothing. Paul looking from one of us to the other like waiting. It was A.J. who broke the silence. With a sudden look of enlightenment on his face he walked forward, reaching out his hand, saying, "Sorry, man."

And Jason followed him, saying, "Me too Tarek," and shook my hand. And I had just about enough sense to realize that I had to answer something like, "Let's forget it, guys," and with that the ritual was over. Then Paul said, "OK, you two clowns clear off home now. Training's tomorrow. See you there." Jason and A.J. got in the truck and drove away. Walking into the house, Paul asked, "Everything OK, Tarek?"

"Yeah," I said, thinking, "I'm OK considering that in the course of the evening I'd been traumatized out of my mind by two lunatic afro-atheists and then hunted like a wild animal through the streets of town by a couple of psychotic killers. I guess I am OK."

"Thanks, Paul," I added, and I think in a way I must have meant it. As we went through the house door, Paul turned to me and held a finger to his lips, saying, "Shhhh," as if to tell me that Heather had slept through the whole thing. He carefully opened the door of their bedroom and then turned around. In a loud whisper, he said across the living room to me: "You gotta understand, Tarek. Something you gotta learn. You go around riling folks like the way you do, some time or another they gonna turn around and strike right back at you fella. They always do."

Preach. Preach. Preach. Preach. Preach.

Don't Let The Sun Set On Him Here

One evening a couple of days later, through the thin wall of my bedroom I could hear Paul talking to his best friend Jimmy. Jimmy was a short, fat, buck-toothed auto mechanic who did a lot of janitor jobs around the church house in his free time. Heather had once hinted that he had something to do with the Klan as a kid. Jimmy had come around unexpected after work and they were both drinking beer in the living room. Jimmy said, "Folks say you gotta be having a lot of trouble with that Muslim boy of yours. That right, Paul?" And Paul answered, "Jimmy, I don't know what's wrong with him. It's like one night he goes to bed like a Christian and the next morning he comes down to breakfast a Muslim. Me and Heather don't understand it all."

"Well Paul," said Jimmy, "that kind of thing don't come across too good in the church community or anywhere else in Shackleton for that matter. You gotta know Paul, people are talking."

Paul sounded exasperated. "Look Jimmy, believe me. We've tried everything. Before he came from Germany he told us, I mean the guy told us that he was a Lutheran Christian and me and Heather were thinking that he'd be like all them fine young Christian kids we saw when we were visiting Eisenach in Germany, where Martin Luther wrote the Bible that time with our Christian student group. And at first he came with us to church and Bible study just like a normal human being. And then this…"

"Yeah, Paul," said Jimmy, "there ain't no explanations for a thing like that…Christian boy becoming a Muslim. Like a car breaking down for no reason on a mountain road or a mad dog baying in the night. But one thing is certain…boy is on the way to Hell."

"Yeah, Jimmy" said Paul, "but you know it kind of appeals to me sometimes the way he defends it all. You know, digs his hills right in. Must take a lot of guts to do what he is doing, alone far from home as he is. Told me yesterday Muslims believe in Jesus and the Virgin Mary, you know that Jimmy?"

"Hey Paul, steady on fella…"

"No Jimmy, really I like the arguments I have with him, all the same."

"Now you listen to me good Paul," said Jimmy in a serious voice, "we've known each other a long time and that's why I'm here. You may like the kid, think he's got big feelings in him, not as big as his mouth maybe, but a real stand-up boy all the same, but you got to understand that there are folks in our community that don't like the situation at all. We being a God fearing Christian town and not needing no Muslim in our midst. You gotta know, Paul, people are starting to talk. Can't you phone the exchange school or whatever it's called, the people in Germany, and send him on back where he came from and they send you someone normal in exchange? That possible Paul? Before this whole thing gets out of hand. Wouldn't like to see you and Heather meeting up with Old Man Trouble 'cause of this."

There was a long pause. It sounded as if Paul had gotten up and was walking around. And then he said, "Jimmy, I guess Minister Riley put you up to this, to come around and have a word with me. Minister Riley and a few other people that I can guess. They all mean well, Jimmy. And I heard it from other quarters as well. School and so on. So has Heather. But we, the pair of us, we got to thinking that we would like to see this thing through. This thing with Tarek. Bring his school year here full to an end like we promised his mother and the folks of the organization. It ain't gonna be easy. But it is like our duty, it's expected from us. We expect it of ourselves. And Jimmy, you got the ear of a lot of the folks out there and you tell them from me, they may not like him, Tarek, but they gotta appreciate that that boy is under my roof and subject to my personal protection during his stay here. Just wanna make that point clear, Jimmy."

After that I couldn't hear any more because they seemed to have moved to the hallway, and I heard the house door close as Jimmy went out into the night. Then I heard Paul going to the kitchen and him and Heather talking. They talked for a long time. I laid on my bed thinking. I felt a vague sense of fear in connection with something that was out there in the streets and houses of Shackleton. Something that was directed against me. Who do they think they are, these kuffar, Paul and Heather? A couple of superheroes?

Sally Jefferson

One day, I was walking along the same way as usual, averting my eyes at the sight of women. On this day I was feeling really, really low and depressed, full of spite. So it was like a gift from heaven that I met at the crossroads opposite the Church House this girl

I knew from school called Sally, Sally Jefferson. Sally was a really slim, fit girl with red hair and freckles who was heavily into yoga and running and calisthenics and other kuffar garbage like that. She happened to be a good listener, so I'd gotten used to using her as a kind of psychic trash can.

"Hi, Tarek."

"Hi, Sally."

"How are you doing, Tarek?"

We sat down together opposite the church on a bench. I was looking at the church with its wooden steeple, which rose to a height of about 100 feet and was therefore the tallest building in that onehorse town. They knew how to attract a man's attention. And I thought this is where I tell a thing or two about Islam. Deepen her knowledge of it. Wake the self-contented airhead up out of her dream world. "Sally," I said turning to her. "This is probably the last time we're gonna see each other. I can't take it anymore. None of it. This place, this town, school, the Millers, the church over there, I am sick of it all. And so I have decided to end it all and go to a better place. Paradise. Tomorrow morning, Sally, I'm gonna come back here after morning prayer with my Quran in my hand and I'm gonna climb up that church steeple over there. And when there are enough folks gathered down here below, I will proclaim the Caliphate of Georgia and then I am gonna cry out with a loud voice, so that all can hear: 'Allahu Akbar!' And then I will kiss the Holy Quran in my hand and I will dive off of that steeple and tomorrow at this time I will be in Paradise with Allah and his angels."

If I'd hoped that this little fantasy would cause her to stop freaking out, begging me in tears not to do it, I was mistaken. She just sat there looking at me with her blue-grey eyes for a while, sort of quizzically, before saying, "How you gonna climb the steeple with your Quran in your hand? That don't sound too good. You gonna have to stick it under your armpit or stuff it down in your pants. Why you looking at me like that, Tarek? Practical aspects of your enterprise got to be addressed. The other thing being, as you know, my dad is Chief of Police here in Shackleton, and he is cruising around all day long in his car looking for serial murderers, Ted Bundy's, guys like that. And if he sees a well-known local Muslim lunatic— in fact, the only one we got in Shackleton— climbing up our steeple with a Quran in his hand, he's gonna think that boy ain't up to nothing good. And he's gonna take his shotgun and blow you right away. Period. End of story."

I was disappointed with her response, but I managed to say something like, "As long as I die for Islam, it will be OK by me." Sally got up and stood in front of me, saying, "Tarek, man, you are one sick, depressed Muslim guy. You all think like that? Like a death cult? Don't you wanna live? Healthy? For as long as possible? Like a normal human being? Look, Tarek, you're depressed, so let's give it for a moment the benefit of the doubt. Maybe it's not this Islam thing, maybe it's your sloppy diet that makes you feel this way. Has it not occurred to you that our Lord Jesus Christ was quite obviously a vegetarian, a fish-eating vegetarian? In the Holy Gospels you only ever see him eating bread, honey, fish, figs, corn, and drinking water or wine. No mention of him actually eating meat at all. Of this I am quite certain." Suddenly she became very thoughtful, scratching her chin and said, almost to herself, "You know, Jesus is the ultimate vegetarian when you come to think of it. Because he is not the one who eats a body but the body who gets eaten." She folded her arms and twirled around full circle, then facing me again smiling, said, "I Tarek, I am named after Sally Jefferson, the wife of our Founding Father Thomas Jefferson, and she is a positive female role model and I intend to be one as well myself. When I finish high school, I am going to NewYork City and there I will find a publisher for my book, it's a cookbook and it's called 'The Jesus Christ Diet Cookbook.' It is a collection of recipes containing figs and wine and fish and bread and honey and water and corn in different combinations, which will lead people to eat healthy and lose weight at the same time as thinking about the life of the Lord. 'The Jesus Christ Diet Cookbook!' Cause you can't be too slim or too Christian. What do you think of that, Tarek? Great, isn't it?"

I just sat there, feigning depression, staring at my feet.

"Better then jumping off a steeple anyway," she said.

I had gotten tired of my charade. I stood up. This was going nowhere with the idiot airhead. But I paused before walking away and forgetting the whole thing, turning and saying to her with fake concern, "Sally, promise me that you won't tell anyone what I intend to do tomorrow."

She shrugged and said, "OK, I won't."

"Promise you won't?" I insisted.

"I won't," she repeated.

"Promise?"

"I won't."

She did.

Twenty Gods or None at All

The next evening when I got home after school, Heather and Paul were waiting for me. As I entered the house I sensed the evil signs. Rommel wasn't around, which meant he'd been locked up. There was no smell of cooking and the television was off. These were not good omens. I went into the living room and I saw Paul und Heather sitting together on the sofa waiting. When she saw me Heather sprung up, her eyes wide open with anger.

"Can you tell me, young man, what in the world was that that you told Sally yesterday?" I'd never seen her in such a rage. Paul was starring wordlessly at me with a look of absolute disgust on his face.

"Yeah…aaa…I know…aaa…. I am…real sorry. It was a mistake." I was hoping that by apologizing quickly, the whole thing would soon be over and I could escape to my room.

"You're sorry!" yelled Heather. "Sorry? Is that all you have to say? What in God's name got into you? How sick are you in your head to be saying stuff like that?"

Paul placed his hand on her shoulder to calm her. "Tarek," he said, "Sally told her mom, her mom called the school, and they called us. Tarek, the whole town, the whole of Shackleton is talking about the lunatic Muslim we got in the house who's gonna kill himself jumping off the church or some nonsense like that."

"The whole town is talking about us. You're shaming us, Tarek, before our neighbors and our friends. Since you come here we've had nothing but trouble with you."

Paul sat down on the sofa, shaking his head. "You lied to us right from the start. You told us you were Protestant."

"Paul, I don't know," I said. "I just put a cross on the form wherever I could to make my chances better of finding an exchange place. I thought seeing that most of you are Protestants here I may as well be one too. That's all." Paul almost exploded. "Listen to me, boy! Religion ain't no hobby, ain't no fad, ain't no Flag of Convenience. For us, our faith is the most important thing in our lives. And you have the nerve and the barefaced audacity to come here into our home claiming to be a Christian and then convert into a Muslim before our eyes on our living room carpet? Who do you think you are? Do you not think that could be a problem for us? For me and Heather?

Did you not think that it might be a problem for the school? For the church down the road that you want to jump off of? That it might be a problem for the whole of this community? For the whole of the state of Georgia? Can you even think at all?" Suddenly I was angry too, and I was thinking: *OK, if this is the way you want it.* "I think you should both understand that all people are born Muslim. No one converts to Islam. We revert. I simply found my way back, praise to Allah, to the true religion of humanity."

Heather, who was near tears, said, shaking her head, "You can say what you like, but me and Paul —we don't believe in your Allah, OK?"

"Because you're too dumb to understand that Allah is just the Arabic for God. It's all the same being," I snapped back.

Paul stood up suddenly, and I backed away to the wall 'cause he looked like he was going ballistic. "Oh really? You think so, fella? You think your God is the same as ours? Your God ain't our God. Your God ain't nothing but some sort of degenerated desert moon God or some lump of stone or rock that you guys be bowing down and praying to." And Heather added, "That's true what Paul says, I read the same in National Geographic."

"You should have read the Quran," I shouted, "Both of you! There you'd read that there is only one God Allah and Mohammed is his prophet."

Paul walked towards me, and I thought that now it would get physical. He pointed his finger at me and said: "Listen, you ain't nothing but a sect and you know what I would do with you all? Whole dumb Islam World…I would nuke you all one after another… I'd start in Senegal, then comes Mauritania, then I'd nuke along the coast of North Africa and right through Egypt and the Middle East, avoiding Israel of course, then I would nuke Turkey and Iran and

Pakistan and I would keep on nuking all the way through till Indonesia, and I would only stop nuking when I had reached the island of Bali because I heard only Hindus and Buddhists and Sikhs live there."

"You're really into National Geographic, ain't you Paul?" I sneered.

Paul lunged closer at me.

"Now listen here, you…"

"OK guys," said Heather, coming between us. "I think that's enough religious discussion for one evening."

She suddenly looked drained. She said, "It's been a long day. I'm tired, I'm sad, and I want to go to sleep. And if you two want to spend the whole night screaming about Christian this and Muslim that, you're welcome to, it but I am going to bed." She walked towards the living room door, but before she left, she turned around and said, "All in all, you know, it's like the man said: "'But it does me no injury for my neighbor to say there are twenty gods or no God. It neither picks my pocket nor breaks my leg.'"

And then she disappeared into the bathroom. Hadn't I heard that somewhere before, I thought? "What man?" I asked Paul. He walked past me and sort of slumped, deflated, into a chair. He looked embarrassed, somehow ashamed. "What man?" I repeated.

"Thomas Jefferson, Founding Father," answered Paul quietly. He looked up at me and said, "Hey Tarek, I guess we should maybe calm down. It's late. We all need some sleep."

That was the first time I experienced something that since then I have experienced again and again. You can be confronted by the loudest, most insulting, obnoxious, redneck type of American you can find. But all you have to do is mention Thomas Jefferson or Thomas Paine or any other Founding Father, asking something like, "What would Thomas Jefferson say if he could hear you tal-

king like that?" and then they'll have their tail between their legs, admitting,
"Aw, gee, shucks, I guess I was out of line." For a long time I thought I had discovered one of their major weaknesses. I didn't know I had discovered one of their greatest strengths.

Shahada

The thing about Sally and the church steeple seemed somehow to blow over. I think the Millers must have been smoothing things over at the school and church. This was fine by me because in my adolescent selfishness I didn't want to get thrown out and sent back to Germany because my private little jihad was simply too much fun. But I felt that I might be living on borrowed time. The Millers might not be able to protect me forever. The kuffar of Shackleton might get real uptight. And then I'd be gone. But if it did come to that I thought that it might be a good idea to make my conversion real official. After everything I had to endure amongst these people in the town of Shackleton, I felt that it was now time to make a clear and positive statement regarding the sincerity of my convictions. Rub their unbelieving noses right into it. And so I decided to find somewhere, anywhere as near as possible, some mosque, a Muslim prayer center or even a solitary Muslim holy man to whom I could see in order to officially speak out the Muslims Declaration of Faith, which is called the Shahada. And it goes, "There is only one God, Allah, and Mohammed is his messenger." So I could always say back in Germany with pride that I had reverted to Islam deep in the Bible Belt, lair of the cursed kuffar. Real cutting edge.

So I went to the public library to look on the internet. There was nothing in Shackleton but I got lucky with Franklin, a town about 50 miles away. Apparently there was something called the "Sayed Qutub Muslim Prayer Center," which seemed to be situated in an industrial area on the edge of town at 100 Francis Drake Street. I

wrote down the address and a couple of days later, I skipped school, went to the bus station, and headed to Franklin. From the bus station in Franklin it took me almost an hour of getting lost to find Francis Drake Street. And I walked along this long, long road with small factories and store rooms and warehouses and auto repair workshops on either side and big trucks passing in both directions. I was really bushed by this time and beginning to think, "What am I actually doing to myself here with this whole self-islamization thing?" Wasn't it supposed to be a joke? Then why am I slogging along this road in the hot, September Georgia sun looking to get really converted? Why am I looking for a mosque in which to do the Shahada? Because it's there, I thought. That's why. Because it's there. After what seemed like an eternity, I got to number 96, a plumbing wholesaler, and then came number 98, a motorbike shop, and then full of excitement and anticipation I ran the last few steps until I was standing outside number 100. I couldn't understand
the world anymore. This couldn't be the "Sayed Qutub Muslim Prayer Center" because what I was looking at was an enormous yard full of stacks of empty beer crates and behind it some sort of halltype building full of alcohol bottles and cans. No Minaret, no prayer room, no muezzin, no brothers and sisters—just alcohol, alcohol and alcohol as far as the eye could see. It wasn't a Mosque, it was an alcohol wholesale depot. I was standing there stunned
and clueless, paralyzed to the spot. Then one of the employees, a big, fat Charles Bukowski-type kuffar with a massive beer belly hanging out of his trousers came out, pushing a pile of beer crates on
a trolly towards a parked truck with the tarpaulin rolled back. He stopped and looked across at me and said, "Hi, about time." He looked back over his shoulder and shouted in the direction of the store hall: "Hey Harv, the customer for the bourbon's here!"
At that moment, I turned to walk away in confusion as Beer Belly came after me, saying, "Hey man, where you going? Your order's

ready!" I stopped and faced him, saying, "Where's the mosque?" He looked at me, puzzled. "Mox? What's mox? You didn't order no mox. You ordered Jack. Fifty boxes of bourbon." I turned and ran right out of the yard and down the street. The big, fat, beer belly kuffar shouting and yelling behind me. I just kept on running through the industrial area back towards the bus station. Tears of anger and frustration and humiliation were pouring down my face. Is this all that this filthy country has to offer by way of Islam? How dare they desecrate a Muslim House of God in that manner. Turn an Islamic prayer center into a dirty, disgusting alcohol warehouse? How dare they? Someone, some upright courageous Muslim man of God, a fearless warrior should surely right this wrong. A holy place defiled with alcohol and occupied by pot-bellied drunks! These vile, worthless, unbelieving scum! This is how they have treated the Muslim world from the beginning! I had never been so angry in this dreadful country until I came to Franklin. Running as fast as I could and gasping for breath and burning with anger within, I ran into the bus station. I could see that my bus already had the engine running and the door was about to close. With a final spurt I made it and the bus driver, another big, fat kuffar, turned at the wheel and asked with an evil grin on his face: "Shackleton?"

Paul's Birthday Present

When I got back to Shackleton an hour or so later, I remembered that it was Paul's birthday. It was the 7th of September. The whole of the Miller family would be there from all over the state, plus all his friends and colleagues from the school and church —virtually everybody he knew in town. It was going to be a big event on account of it being Paul's 40th birthday. I realized walking through the town that I hadn't gotten around to buying the moron a birthday present. Seeing that I was still in a state of anger after what had happened to the mosque and everything in Franklin I went straight to the book

shop on Hugh Dowding Street and bought him a big deluxe Quran in English. Sitting on the sidewalk outside, I wrote on the flyleaf:
"Happy Birthday, Paul, I hope that you will discover the truth of Islam and become a decent Muslim before it's too late, Inshallah. Yours, Tarek." I had been hoping that I could drop the bombshell about my Shahada at the party in front of everybody, not that it would have made much sense to them. But even this pleasure had been denied to me now.
I took my time getting there. I spent some time just drifting around the streets. Hanging out here and there. Some inner instinct telling me that maybe I should calm down some before going to the house. When I eventually got there I could see from the garden that the house was full. I could see Paul's parents through the window. And also Minister Riley. I went in reluctantly. Rommel jumped up at me barking, and I pushed him away. The whole of Shackleton
seemed to be present. Most of the church, most of Paul's colleagues from school, lots of friends of Heather's, lots of neighbors, and the whole of Paul's filthy football team, including my arch enemy, the sick maker himself, Jason. Paul was a really popular guy in town. Heather had obviously done a great deal of work fixing up a really big buffet in the middle of the room and there was music playing: Lynard Skynyrd, Dollie Parton, rubbish like that. Everybody was congratulating Paul and he was smiling the whole time all over his big, dumb face. The Birthday Boy. At one stage a couple of geeks from church sang some sort of Christian song to guitars, the
usual stuff about Lord and Jesus. And suddenly Jimmy was standing in front of me, Paul's nasty friend, the one that had been hinting a couple of weeks ago that a Shackleton lynch mob was thinking about bull whipping me to death in the street at some point. I could see that he was completely drunk. Big, red face and eyes glazed with bourbon. Jack, I thought. 50 boxes.
And Jimmy was saying, "Hey, look what we got here everybody. If

it ain't our raghead friend, Shackleton's own Mr. Malcom X. Direct from the gutters of Cairo, Egypt, the one and only Tarek Waleed. Where's your camel, boy? Tied up outside?"

I could hear Jason laughing out loud nearby. I said to Jimmy, "Man, you're drunk. Just leave me alone. What did I do to you?"

"Listen, Bedouin boy," said Jimmy, "folks around here had enough of you and this Muslim talk you been laying on them all the time. 'Bout time you learned who got the say in this town before somebody reach across and knock some of the sand outta your head. You ain't gonna know whether to wash your feet or roll your prayer mat!"

"You know, Jimmy," I said, "I've been told that here in the USA everyone has the right to be a dirty, lowlife piece of racist hillbilly white trash, but you are abusing the privilege."

"Wow! Listen to the Muslim college sand nigg…"

Joyce, who was a friend of Heather, jumped in between us, saying, "Hey, calm down, you guys crazy or what? Wouldn't it be better if we were all to drink
a toast to Paul? Like we're here to do? Huh? Jimmy? Think you've had a bit too much to drink."

The whole room had gone quiet and was looking towards us. "Yeah Jimmy, sit down," said someone. "Leave the guy alone," said someone else. Jimmy walked across the room, away from me, and sat down next to Jason. Jason whispered something in his ear and they both looked across at me, grinning.

Heather walked up towards me, handing me a glass of orange juice, and said with a smile: "Some guys just can't handle their drink, Tarek." I set the glass down on the table next to me and looked around the room. Jimmy and Jason had now been joined by Minister Riley and they were all smirking in my direction. And then I snapped.

"You all make me sick!" I bellowed at the whole room. "The whole time I've been here you've been insulting my religion. All of you. I've had enough of your dumb comments. All you Americans are the same. You're ignorant, backwards, retarded, you know nothing, nothing at all about other people, other cultures. You live like you are living on the moon!"

"We were on the moon," said somebody, and the whole room laughed.

"You should have stayed there! Been better for the world. For humanity, if you just weren't around. You all think that you are the best, better than everyone else and you spread yourselves around and trample with your cowboy boots on the whole world. What right do you think you have to tell us all what to do? How we should live? How we should think? Your whole land was built on crime, on slavery, on mass murder and it doesn't worry you at all. You think the whole world belongs to you and everything in it and you can just go out and take it with war and brute force."

They were all just sitting there and staring at me blankly. I had the feeling that I was slowly losing control over myself.

"I just wanna say this." I went on, feeling the anger surging within me: "What are you doing to the Indians? To the black Americans? Shoot 'em on the street or pack 'em in prison. You racist pack! Rosa Parks herself said the whole misery of the world is down to you. You and your predator capitalism, your murder banks on Wall Street, your Goldman Sachs, peculating in basic food commodities, and the children in the Third World dying of hunger because of it. A Holocaust day for day, year for year! Your Coca-Cola imperialism and your almighty dollar oppressing the people of the planet, and anyone who doesn't play along gets bombed and napalmed till they get back in line. You're drowning in blood. You've no idea how people like me and the rest of the world despise you!" And I leaned forward and spat on the floor in front of them. They all just sat there, some looking shocked, some just looking at the floor. Paul was shaking his head, looking sad, and Heather like she might burst into tears. This just made me angrier:

"Criminals! That's what you are. Telling the whole world a load of baloney about human rights then trampling them into the ground so that you can set up your New World Order for your Freemason bankers and Illuminati. Hiroshima! Vietnam! Agent Orange! You played football with the heads of Viet Cong children! I despise your whole culture. Your military and your greed for gold and oil. You spread lies about Muslim people in order to steal their wealth and kill them. You killed hundreds of thousands of them. In Iraq, in Iran, all over. Because you feel deep down inside that Islam is the only power on earth that can oppose you. That's why you come to our lands and make war against Muslims.

You think I am the only one who thinks like this? I could show you a couple of guys in Frankfurt, in Germany, who think the same as me. People who are of my mind in every backyard mosque in Hamburg, in Berlin, in Cologne. How long's it gonna be before you bomb holy Mecca itself?" I stood back, took a deep breath, and screamed from the top of my voice: "But we're gonna get you first! The Muslims are coming! Allahu Akbar! You unbelievers! Your days are numbered! Listen to me good, you kuffar of Shackleton: Death is on its way! You godless pagans and venomous wretches! Hell and its fire is yawning for you all and will swallow you up!"

And then I took the Quran out of my rucksack and tore off the gift paper, saying, "Here Paul, here is your birthday present. Maybe you get to die with a Quran in your hand—catch!" And I threw the book across the room at him.

And then I said, "One thing I promise you. One thing I promise you all. Mark my words carefully! One day my Muslim brothers will come to your country in airplanes and they will blow up your houses, your families, your children, and your skyscraper buildings till you can never rebuild them again. Allahu Akbar!" That's what I said. I walked out of that silent room and into my bedroom, slamming the door as hard as I could and exhausted, lied myself down on the bed that Heather had freshly changed for me a couple of hours before.

The Morning After the Night Before

I woke up the next morning. It was real late. For a split second I had a smile on my face. Then I remembered the night before. No one had come to wake me. I lay there for some time. The house was completely quiet. I got up and went into the living room. Not even Rommel was there. There were a few traces still of the party the night before, but not much, as if it had all broken up early and they had time to clear things away. There was no breakfast as usual, but on the table there was a note. It was from Heather. It said: "Tarek, it's best you don't go to school today. Just stay at home, please. We'll all see each other this evening. Heather."

I never knew a day that went by so slowly. I watched some TV. Slept a bit on the sofa. Couldn't eat much. Hour after hour just crawled by. I was thinking, what is going to happen now? I was beginning to feel more than a little uneasy. Kind of scared. What will they do to me? Round about 4 o'clock in the afternoon I heard Heather's car pull into the driveway and Rommel barking. I sat up on my chair as she came in. I didn't know what to say.

"Hi Tarek," she said, sort of embarrassed. "Look… mmh…Paul is gonna be late this evening. There is like a meeting at school." She started smoothing cushions on the sofa, absently, and then she said, "You may as well know, Tarek, I suppose you can guess it's about you." She seemed to be under pressure. "The people from church are there as well and the PTA. Lot of folks. Yeah. We just have to wait till Paul comes. I'll make us something to eat, OK?" I said not-

hing. I didn't have anything to say. Heather scratched a meal together and we ate it in silence. Afterwards, I played around a bit half-heartedly with Rommel. I would have liked to have turned the TV on by way of diversion, but it didn't seem right. Long day, long evening. Round about 8:30 Paul's car came into the driveway. Paul came into the house, Rommel jumping up at him. I saw Paul and Heather exchange glances. I was sitting on the sofa and Paul slumped into the armchair opposite me. He looked real tired. Drained. I had never seen him so burnt out before. He looked up at me and then said, "We don't have to talk about last night. Forget it. Heather must have told you about the meeting just now at school. What can I say, Tarek? I'd be lying to you if I would say that there ain't a lot of bad feelings toward you around here. There were a lot of people there. Yeah, whole lot of people. Most of them not wanting you around here no more. Most of them I've known most of my life. There was a lot of hard things said. But I know these folks here. You can talk to them. If you know them well enough, that is. What it all comes down to is this: It's gonna be alright, Tarek. No one's gonna send you away. You're gonna finish your year here. Nothing's changed. It's gonna be alright. You're gonna carry on going to school and living here with me and Heather. Just like we promised your mom." He looked down at the floor for a moment and then looked up and said with a small smile: "It's gonna be OK, Tarek. We're gonna see this thing through. Together. You and me and Heather." He stood up and said, "What do you say, Tarek, sound good to you?" and stretched out his hand. "Wanna shake on it? What do you think?"
I looked at him and I thought: Him with his smug little Christian do-gooder smile on his face, thinks he's doing his godly duty and me a big favor at the same time and feeling oh-so-good about it. So I said, "What do I think, Paul? I think you make me sick! I've had it with you all and your Baptist dogoodery. It makes me wanna throw up! Keep it! It's over! I am out of here. Gone. I want the next plane

back to Frankfurt now! Fix it Paul! Do me just one last favor, seeing you're so good at that. Fix it!" Paul looked at me in dismay for a couple of seconds and then sat down on the chair and seemed to shrivel up inside himself. I had the feeling he would never speak again. He was looking at me with complete hopelessness. Behind me, I could hear Heather saying, "Oh no."

Then Paul said in a low voice, so quiet I could hardly hear him: "Ok Tarek…if that's the way you want it."

Homeward Bound

Heather got everything organized quickly. The next morning she called a friend who worked at Atlanta Airport and got my plane ticket changed for the following day. I spent the day hanging around the house and packing my things together. And I called my mom in Frankfurt and told her I was coming home. Things hadn't worked out. It was a Sunday. The Millers went to church as usual, and I imagine they told everybody that I was leaving. Good news travels fast. Heather and Paul came home after church, and the rest of the day went by slowly; a day of clammy Georgia heat. We didn't talk much. There wasn't anything left to say.

Early the next morning after a night of thunder and lighting, Paul and Heather drove me to the small airport outside Shackleton. After days of unbearable heat, the storm in the night had cooled everything down. In the car, to break the silence, Heather asked me, "Is it far? In Frankfurt. From the airport to your house, I mean?" "No." I was beginning to feel bad about the whole thing. To be leaving like this. And everything. Paul drove the whole way without saying a word, just concentrating on the road. At the airport parking lot I got out of the truck and went to get my luggage out of the back. Paul pushed me aside, saying, "I'll do that." He walked in front of Heather and me carrying the two suitcases in each hand. All I had in my hand was the lunchbox that Heather had packed for me be-

fore we left. I'd already started to feel kind of sad in the car and now it was getting worse as I watched Paul walking along across the parking lot carrying my heavy luggage, just like he'd been carrying the burden of me as a person all these months past. After the check-in we walked to the departure gate and the moment of farewell had come. "OK, Tarek, take care of yourself," said Paul briskly, and gave me a quick, firm handshake and stepped back. Heather put her arms around me and wished me a good flight and all the best for my future. I walked to the end of the corridor and despite myself turned around again. They were both still standing there just looking in my direction. And I thought, "Look at them, the two kuffars." I showed them. They would remember me. The last I saw of them was Heather waving at me and smiling a forced smile. Paul stood next to her, his shoulders hanging down, looking at the floor like a soldier who failed to accomplish his mission. I waved back, turned, and boarded the plane.
As the plane taxied along the runway I started to feel badly again about leaving and the way I'd behaved over the months. But then I thought, "So what?" Just forget the whole thing. Put it behind you. Forget it. It's over.
I flew from Atlanta to Frankfurt and got to Falkstraße at 4 o'clock in the morning. I talked a little to mom, but after pleading jet lag, went to bed. Back home with mom again. I fell asleep. I was woken nine hours later by my mom shaking me awake. She was freaking out:
"Tarek, wake up! Wake up! Something terrible is happening!" and ran out of the room. Shocked, I followed her. She was standing in the living room, staring at the television. For the rest of the day I watched live on German television the events in New York on the 11th of September, 2001.

Germany, Hamburg, Egypt, Islam, Suicide, Djihad, planes flying into buildings, the people jumping out of the burning windows of the World Trade Center, the buildings collapsing, the firemen, the

Dust Lady, 3500 dead…
ASSHOLE, ASSHOLE, ASSHOLE, ASSHOLE,
ASSHOLE, ASSHOLE, ASSHOLE, ASSHOLE,
ASSHOLE, ASSHOLE, ASSHOLE, ASSHOLE…
I felt like I wanted the earth to just swallow me up; I simply wanted to die out of shame.

After the 11th of September

In the following days I wanted to phone Paul and Heather to apologize for everything but I didn't have the courage. The minutes, the hours, the days, the weeks went by and in the end, 16 years have gone by and I still haven't called. During all these years, every time I heard or thought about the 11th of September, I felt sick to my stomach because I associated it with how I had behaved in Shackleton towards Paul and Heather and everyone else. It was as if I was guilty as well, somehow connected with the terror on that day in New York. I'd lay awake at night and see the accusing eyes and faces in the room at Paul's birthday party.

It frightened me to think what the people there would have thought of me after the attack. How did they react to Paul and Heather? They'd defended me, after all. At the same time, I knew that I was lucky to have gotten out of there just one day before. The days after 9/11 weren't a good time to be a Muslim in the US. What would have happened to a Muslim like me who said the things I said? I decided to try to suppress the whole thing, forget it all as if it had never happened. I wasn't there, it wasn't me, it wasn't them. Tarek Waleed was never in Shackleton. Just a bad dream. Naturally, this didn't work very well. There were always moments when it all came back, like late in the evenings when I'd think of it or when I felt compelled to dig out their photos or look at them years later on Facebook. Yes, I followed them secretly online and of course over the years 9/11 was repeatedly referred to and every time I heard of

9/11 I was sick to my stomach, consumed by my shame and guilt. It was almost as if somehow I was one of the perpetrators myself. I felt like I was personally responsible. And in all those years, I didn't get it together to phone the Millers; like a murderer, I blocked all avenues that led to me.

I was just a dirty little coward. I couldn't even look the people in my photos from Shackleton in the eyes. It was that bad. So what did happen next? My life just went on. I lived with Mom in Frankfurt, finished high school, and started studying for a law degree at the Johann Wolfgang Goethe University, also in Frankfurt. The major reason for this was that when I unpacked my bags that day in Frankfurt after getting home from Shackleton, I found a copy of *To Kill a Mockingbird* that Heather must have slipped in my bags before I left. I actually read it and was fascinated by the character and role of Atticus Finch. It sort of inspired me. I began to fantasize that I too could become a heroic criminal defense lawyer.

This led to a sort of parallel course of study to my legal studies. I remembered all the books in the Miller's house. Some of the titles and some of the authors had stuck in my memory, and I set about finding them. By chance, outside the university in Frankfurt there were several used bookr stands. One of these was a washed-up English guy called John who was from Coventry, England, and who only sold books in English. I asked him one day if he had any books by Tom Paine. I remember the look on his face, as if I had fallen from heaven. The first books I bought from him were *The Age of Reason* and *The Rights of Man*. Over the years he supplied me with books by Emerson, Thoreau, Godwin, Orwell, and so on and so on…until I think I had virtually replicated the Miller's library in my room in Bockenheim. The centuries-old, radical, enlightening, organically growing, collective ideas of the Anglosphere. This parallel world of free-thinking accompanied me all those years, shaping me imperceptibly. And while I was reading it, I also felt in a strange sort of way close to the Miller's, my lost friends, so far away. Like I was sitting next to them, sharing it with them, growing with them.

Future Legislators of Society

During my law studies I found a girlfriend, Hannah, a happy-go-lucky girl who looked like the actress Sandra Bullock, along with a couple of friends, Osman, and his girlfriend, Jusra. We were all studying law together. Hannah was German from Mainz, and Nusra and Osman were like myself: the children of immigrants. Jusra's parents came from Syria and Osman's were from Turkey. They were both devout Muslims. Osman was the vainest man I had ever met. He wore a suit, had a perfectly trimmed beard, and was extremely opinionated, about everything. Jusra always wore expensive silk headscarves and liked to present herself as the perfect western Muslim lady. Both of them were very popular and charismatic with obviously bright futures. They seemed like examples of a perfect assimilation, balancing western and Islamic values wonderfully. Each year Hannah, Osman, Jusra and I went together on vacation. Normally we went to Turkey or Tunisia. Hannah was basically unpolitical. We talked about other things, normal things. That's how she was, and my mom really liked her. The perfect future daughter-in-law. A career wife and mother, uncomplicated. I should have noticed something strange about Osman and Jusra. Every time when I would go on about American democracy, freedom, and enlightenment, they never gave their own opinions. They would always say, "You're right, Tarek. Very interesting." Whenever I talked with enthusiasm about The Founding Fathers and freedom of opinion, they would just smile and answer in bored voices: "You should become a politician." They both seemed to be more interested in organizing their Ramadan fasts and a Muslim prayer room in our institute. Once, I said to Osman that the concept of Human Rights conceived by the

West was the greatest ever in history: "Isn't the sentence 'All men are created equal' absolutely great?" He just smiled silently at me in response. I should have noticed that something was wrong with them, both of my muster Muslim friends, with their German passports, smart suites, and silk scarves and perfect manners. I liked to think they were liberal, reform-type Muslims like my dead friend Mo would have turned out to be. An Islam for the 21st century. Yet, whenever I brought these things up with them I should have noticed that there was a wall between us. What was behind this wall I discovered years later, in Berlin. Jusra and Osman married during the course of their studies. They told Hannah and me that it was their families' wish. Hannah thought it a bit strange that the incentive should come from their families and not from them. But I said nothing. I kind of knew the deal. Like, you don't suppose to live like German kuffar? Hannah was always just great. She really had patience with me shooting off my mouth about politics and so on, at parties and at university. And in the buses and street cars in Frankfurt. I'd only told her half of the truth about what happened in Shackleton. She never pressed me about it, although she must have sensed that something was bugging me about that time but probably thought I'd get over it.

Trojan Horses

"I wouldn't put a foot in there," said Osman vehemently. And his wife said the same: "Never in a million years." It was a broiling hot summer's day in the middle of July. The four of us were visiting Berlin for the weekend with a group of other law students on a course trip, and we were all standing in front of the Jewish Museum in Berlin. We'd already visited the Bundestag—the German Parliament, the Brandenburger Tor, Checkpoint Charlie, Schloss Bellevue, the German president's residence, and so on. And now we were standing in front of the Jewish Museum, the biggest museum for Jewish culture and Holocaust history in the center of the city. I suggested that we go in and visit it with the rest of the group who were already inside. "But why not?" I asked, "What's wrong with you?"

"Tarek," said Osman, you serious? You really want us to go in and waste our time on this Jewish selfpity number? What kind of a Muslim are you?"

"What are you talking about?" I asked.

And Jusra said, "You know what Jews do to Muslims, Tarek, or not? Always these Germans with their guilt thing."

"No wonder," said Osman, "that the whole world hates Jews. What with their continual propaganda bleating about what was done to them."

"Whole cities here in Germany have got memorial stones stuck in the sidewalks and plaques on every wall all about the poor, poor little Yahudis and the wrong that was done to them," said Jusra. We`re sick of it" said Osman.

"Osman I think…"

"Tarek!" Osman broke in. "Me and Jusra ain't going to do the penitent kuffar pilgrimage trip. Millions do it…not us!"

"Why not?" I asked, laughing.

"Because the Holocaust never happened," said Jusra, "that's why. Jews are the biggest criminal going. Look at Palestine."

"We wouldn't pay a cent to see their lying show," said Osman. "Did you know that on the 11th of September there were no Jews in the World Trade Center? All set up between them and the CIA so that they could have a go at us Muslims."

And his wife added, "When the kuffar jumped out of the windows, it was like they were falling into Hell." Osman laughed.

Hannah grabbed me by the arm. She was really uptight: "Are you all crazy? Gone mad, or what? Talking like this on the street in this heat. What'll people think? Tarek, I'm not going to hang around here till you're done, I'm going inside with the others."

Although I was really shocked and angry at Osman and Jusra and what they were saying, I left it because of Hannah and we went inside. Osman and Jusra went somewhere else. The whole time we were in the museum I couldn't concentrate on the exhibits. It had nothing to do with my ADHS; it was because of those two and the way they had seemed to suddenly show their true colors. Pure Muslim hatred of Jews. All of it handed down to them from their parents and families over generations. Repeating it like parrots. The same garbage that my family had tried to dump on me. Had they learned nothing? Just the same old hate, hate, hate against the USA and Jews. Same old brainwash. I'd had it with them. Despite their law studies, perfect German, and cultivated exteriors, Osman and Jusra obviously had the same mindset as my uncle Murad and his likes in Cairo all those years ago, and the Terror Sheikh as well. It had become clear to me that Osman and Jusra, like so many others like them, were just Trojan horses: on the outside, decent upstanding people, but seething religious fanatics inside.

We all met again in the evening in our hotel, and for Hannah's sake I tried to talk to them normally and friendly. They bought themselves designer shades and Osman got a new designer watch. It gave me satisfaction to see how much they liked western consumer goods. I'd seen this of course often enough amongst the Muslims of Frankfurt and elsewhere.

Oh, how they all loved designer watches, handbags, shoes, iPhones, laptops, flashy cars, medical care, and all the other conveniences, discoveries, and benefits of western society. But oh, how they ignored and rejected the western values that go with them (or should).

Later that evening the four of us were sitting together in the hotel bar. Osman was playing with his new watch. Nobody was saying anything. There seemed to still be some tension between us, so I tried to start a conversation to break the ice: "Did you see the posters for the mayor of Berlin election? They're all over the city."

"I couldn't care less," said Jusra. "I never vote for them," said Osman, grinning at me. He obviously could sense my aggression towards him from earlier.

"If everybody thought like you, there'd be no democracy."

"Leave it Tarek!" said Hannah. "Don't start all that again."

But Osman clearly didn't want to leave it. He'd been waiting for this opportunity for years: "Listen Tarek, you're always talking about the responsibility of the individual in this society. But you know what? I despise German society. All that counts for a Muslim is his family and his Islamic community. Nothing else. This German society of yours lets its old people, its parents, rot in Old People's Homes. That's not how it is in Islamic society. You're always going on about democracy and the German constitution and how you're going to become a poor man's lawyer. But you know what, Tarek? This country means nothing to me. I want to become a lawyer and earn as much as I can to enrich my family. But this land and its constitution interests me as much as the dirt on my shoes. Aren't you ashamed, Tarek, as a Muslim whose father came from Egypt, when you say you're proud to be German? What is that but a betrayal
of your family and your religion? Wake up, Tarek! You'll never be accepted by the Germans as a German. You'll always be whatever you achieve, a dirty little Arab."

"Osman is right," said Jusra. "You know what they're like." She looked across to Hannah, embarrassed for a moment, but then pulled herself together. I'd always had the feeling that with her headscarves she felt morally superior to Hannah and all other German women.

She let her hatred out: "The German couple like animals when they have a few beers. And their women with their high heels walking around half-naked, looking like hookers. They go naked like dogs in the sauna. No religion, no God, just booze, food, and sex. Nothing else. You think we'll let our son or daughter marry one of them?"
"As a Muslim, I say democracy is blasphemy," said Osman.

Shocked, I looked across at Hannah. Hannah said nothing. She took out her iPhone and began checking her email or something, detached. Hannah, like my mother and virtually all Germans, are masters of suppression. Unpleasant facts concerning Islamism or Neonazism, even when they are directly in front of their noses, are simply ignored, not talked about. Because people don't talk about things like that, do they? Osama bin Laden could rise from the dead and blow himself up in front of the Brandenburger Tor in Berlin and the people would just say: "Where can we get a nice cheeseburger?" Total indifference battened down with arrogance. And this is what allows the likes of my two Muslim Trojan horse friends to enjoy the benefits of western society and snicker behind their hands at each atrocity. Muslim Schadenfreude.

The Dark Ladies of Cairo

Because of my ADHD, my studies were taking a long time—even longer than the normal German study time, which is long. Just after the Arab Revolution and the fall of Mubarak and the election of the Muslim Brotherhood in a fair election by the majority of the people in accordance with the highest standards of international electoral observation, I began as part of my law studies an internship at the German Chamber of Commerce in Cairo. Cairo had changed for me a lot. It was no longer the mysterious city of the Arabian Nights that it was for me as a child. The Egyptian military were in control preelection. I was really, really glad to be walking around with a German passport in my pocket. For here the climate was explosive.

Chaos ruled despite the army. The strongest ruled. Crime was rampant. A young kid was murdered who lived not far away from me. He'd gotten involved in some criminal thing and had been chopped up and thrown into the Nile. Policemen had formed gangs to rob tourists. Even as a Westerner it was better to have nothing to do with the cops or authorities. Even just to be a Westerner was dangerous. A young American student, Andrew Pochter, was stabbed to death by a mob on the Tahrir Square for taking photos. Everywhere I seemed to sense hatred against the West and Americans. A dark brooding culture of hate and violence.

I was staying with my Egyptian family, so at home I was safe enough, and at work, but whenever I walked around the streets I could feel people's eyes watching me. Despite my Arab appearance, they could sense something different about me, and didn't seem to like it much. Only what was conformist seemed to be accepted; anything else was despised. If you were riding in a taxi as a Westerner, you'd be given the third degree: "You, Amriki? You English? You married? How many children? You Muslim? You Christian?" I'd never experienced so much racism and prejudices as in those three months. I would have liked to have said to all my big, fat Cairo cab drivers: "I'm a gay Jewish atheist and I'm on my way to visit my Coptic boyfriend who I met in Israel." But I never did for the simple reason that I was afraid most of the time. As always, my German student colleagues who I'd met there never spoke about all this. Masters of suppression.

Then one evening, at a party in an expats flat-share in the Zamalek district, I met Nicole. She was an Oriental Studies student from Berlin doing an Arabic language course. Nicole was wearing wide, yogatype pants with Hindu symbols on it. She had bright red hair in dreadlocks, a real post-hippie airhead. She told me she'd been in India, Thailand, and Nepal, searching for the truth. Ashrams and gurus and so forth. Now, in Cairo, she was rambling on about the mystical Orient and the poet Rumi and Islamic calligraphy and so on. She said she found the human warmth in Egypt between people totally cool. Airhead! She said, "Their kindness, Tarek, is unlimited. They tell you about Islam and wow, they can even arrange a marriage so you don't have to be alone. Isn't that great, Tarek?" I was thinking that outside on the streets people were being arrested, tortured, and murdered, and she didn't seem to notice at all. Or if she did, it didn't bother her much in her soap bubble. "Listen, Nicole," I said to her urgently. "You're making a big mistake…"

But we were interrupted, and I lost sight of her that evening. A couple of weeks later I met her again. For the second and last time. It was evening and already dark. I met her on some street near Tahrir Square. We were standing underneath a shimmering yellow street light.

"Hey, Tarek," she said happily. "How are you? Things OK?"

"Not really."

"Why not?"

"Nicole, I don't think you'd really understand," I said, because I'd noticed that her hippie clothes were gone and she was dressed in a long, black garment and wearing a black head scarf. Things seemed to have taken a terrible direction with her. She'd found what she was looking for.

"Tarek, I don't understand, you're Egyptian. Muslim. Or not? Coming here from Germany you must feel….like coming home."

"This isn't home. This place is like a prison. No one is free here. I can't breathe."

"My sisters in the mosque tell me that only in our hearts we can be free."

She was drowning, I thought, this little airhead from Berlin, and she wasn't even waving. She was a good person. She'd been searching for the truth, and what had she found? I swear if only I'd had the time I would have….but at that moment from out of the darkness near Tahrir Square, two women in black nikabs appeared and walked up to us. They ignored me, saying to Nicole in English: "Sister, what are you doing here? We think its better that you come with us now."

Nicole said, "Tayeb, OK," then turned around without speaking to me and walked away across the road with a woman on each side. As they reached the other side of the street, I saw emerging from the shadows a large group of silent, black-shrouded, nikab-wearing women and Nicole. The two women disappeared amongst them, the whole group vanishing into the darkness. I never saw her again.

Here Comes the Judge

Just before my bar exam, I was in a lecture in the Department of Justice in Frankfurt. This was part of the final preparation phase and we were attending a lecture on Civil Law. Our lecturer was a practicing judge at the Civil Court in Frankfurt, a very important person. Plenty of influence, greatly respected, author of several textbooks—an expert in his field. His name was Dr. Adolf von Reich. He was in his mid-50s with a pockmarked face, thin hair, a bulbous nose, and looked like he was no stranger to the booze. There were 15 other students present apart from me and Hannah and Osman and Jusra. We were sitting in a large room, in a rundown postwar building, in a half-horseshoe formation around von Reich, who was seated in front of us on a podium. The fact that the subject matter was absolutely boring wasn't helped by von Reich's conceited and arrogant manner. He loved to include in his lectures personal stories of his great performances, his cleverness, and so on in his professional life. I believe that he and I hated each other on sight.

He was a typical German legal type—elitist, snobbish, and condescending—and it was well-known that he was as a young man active in right-wing student fraternities and was now close to certain shadowy Neofacist circles. Up to now it had been a completely routine day. And then it happened.

"Ladies and gentlemen, a word of warning," said Dr. von Reich on reaching the end of his lecture. "Should you, through lack of ability, fail in your final exams, then you should be aware that your fate will be like so many other failed law students: you'll be condemned to spend the rest of your lives working in an obscure legal department of a mediocre firm in some low clerical capacity. The penalty for failure is that you will become the Office Niggers of our profession." I'd heard it, but I didn't believe it. Did he say it? He said it. He really said it. And he just sat there, smiling at us as if he said a really clever thing. Nobody said anything.

He began to speak again: "So, it is in your best interest…"

I hesitated for a moment and looked around me, but still no one had said anything. No reaction at all. And then the tinnitus started ringing in my ear, my present from the Gauland Twins, my little Nazi friends. And before I knew where I was, I was standing up and I was saying, "Excuse me, Dr. von Reich, but do you really think that the word you just used is appropriate for a man in your position in the times that we live in?" There was an absolute dead silence in the room. And I knew just standing there that my life was as good as over. I was finished. As good as dead.

"I beg your pardon, Mr. Waleed?" he asked, fixing me with a look that froze the blood in my veins. I knew I should have stopped, apologized, and sat down. My future was at stake, and this man was really powerful. He made and broke careers. It was madness to make an enemy of him, but then a wave of anger hit me, and I said, "You used the N-Word. You said it in English, Dr. von Reich. It is the worst word of racist insult to black people there is. People don't talk like that." He continue staring at me, saying nothing. None of my fellow students spoke either. There was a total silence in the room, giving me the feeling that I had made a terrible mistake. The atmosphere in the room strangely reminded me of the atmosphere in the Millers' living room when I flipped out during Paul's birthday party. What's wrong with me, I thought? Why do I do these things? Why do I lash out like this? Mess my life up?

"Mr. Waleed," said Dr. von Reich with a poisonous smile, "are you insinuating that I am a racist?"

There were a few giggles from the group. They were enjoying this. Hannah, who was sitting next to me, was kicking me frantically on the shin under the table. But I couldn't stop.

"You use a word like that in the US or Britain, and today would be your last day as a judge."

"May I point out to you, Mr. Waleed, that we are not in the USA or Britain. We are in Germany, and I may express myself as I please. Is that clear?"

"There are universal standards of behavior, sir. Simply because you are in a position of authority here doesn't give you the right to say what you like."

He looked at me as if I was an insect. "Now, Mr. Waleed, let me make one thing perfectly clear…"

For the next ten minutes, for the obvious pleasure of the people around me (with the exception of Hannah), he delivered a tirade of abuse against me, summoning up all the rhetorical skills of an experienced judge. It was really destructive and I've forgotten most of it. A lot of it seemed to be about the American military occupation of Germany and the imposing of American culture on the German people, resulting in idiots like me. There was also a lot of stuff about making us all feel guilty about our past and American political correctness destroying the right to think. I noticed that this was coming across really well and that most of the group was looking at Dr. von Reich with their eyes shining in admiration. And there I was, still standing there on display. I had never felt so alienated from the country of my birth in my life. I had made a laughingstock of myself. As we left the room nobody even looked at me, but they all had smiles on their faces. Smiles of…there is a German word for it, but no equivalent in English: Schadenfreude. It means something like taking pleasure in the discomfort of others. It is a national characteristic. I always think that it is a plus point that people of the Anglosphere have no word for it.

Hannah came running down the street after me. She was livid. I'd never seen her so angry. She said, "Are you stupid or crazy or what? Do you know who that is? What influence he has? You realize you've probably just destroyed your career? I've had it with you, Tarek, and your mouthing off all over the place. Do you know how embarrassing that is? I am sick to death of it—Jefferson, Paine, Finch and the rest of the garbage you come out with. If you want to mess your life up then do it but you won't be dragging me down with you. It's over! Don't call or talk to me again."

I tried to say something but she just walked away, leaving me standing there in the middle of the street.

Frankfurt Railway Station

Naturally, I did try to get in touch with Hannah, but it was no use. She simply ignored me. Didn't answer the phone and avoided me in public, as did the rest of my class. It was obvious that it was over, which was pretty hard as we'd been together for five years. So I decided to concentrate on my final bar exam and shut it all out. I decided to compensate for all of this by showing them all and becoming a great legal advocate, someone along the lines of Atticus Finch or Clarence Darrow. That would show them, I thought. They'd all be sorry they had treated me the way they had. My big mouth would serve me well in the court room. Standing on the shoulders of Mr. Finch and Mr. Darrow. And so I studied night and day cramming for my final state exam. However, at the back of my mind the whole time was the sneaking fear that Dr. von Reich (who was now my sworn enemy) might do something against me regarding the results. Did his influence really reach so far? I tried to write it off as paranoia. I took my final state exam, then waited three months for the results. They arrived by post in a yellow envelope. I'd failed. 10 years of studying for nothing.

And that was it with Tarek Waleed, Star Lawyer, successor of Atticus Finch and Clarence Darrow. The best that I could hope for now with the intermediary qualification was exactly what Dr. von Reich had prophesied for the likes of me: a job behind a desk in some meaningless insurance company assessing claims. He would laugh long and loud when he heard of it, if indeed he hadn't caused it. He was vindictive enough.

In the following days, despite the concern of my mother, I hid myself away in my room and avoided contact with everyone. I'd had it with the world and everyone in it. I only ventured out to the supermarket on the Leipziger Straße each day to stock up on cans of cheap beer, which I guzzled down one after the other. The days passed in a haze of drunkenness and self-pity. One Friday evening I was drunk enough—and yet sober enough—to realize I ought to do something. I had to get out of there. Halfdrunk, I decided to go to Frankfurt Railway Station, where I'd heard that every Friday evening in a coffee shop called "Carminez" inside the railway station, Hannah, Osman, and Jusra, along with other former fellow students of mine, liked to meet at the end of the week to talk shop. They were all by now young lawyers, working for law firms in and around Frankfurt, well into the first stage in their professional lives. I was half hoping that my old clique would have some kind of sympathy for me and provide a bit of support. Maybe we could all get along again. So I left the house and headed for the railway station. It was cold, bleak, there were dark rain clouds hanging in the sky, and I didn't know that I was on the way to my salvation.

I walked along my street, Falkstraße, where I was born, where I grew up. I walked past the home of my old school friend, The Great David Rosenberg. I thought again how odd it was that an entire Jewish family could just disappear like that from out of the middle of the neighborhood without anybody noticing or caring. I walked on to the tower at Bockenheimer Warte, where good, old, fat, mystical Tony saw his vision of the Queen of Heaven, and then I was standing at the entrance of the university next to John's book stand, like a thousand times before. Although it was early evening and no one was there, as usual, drunkenness and sheer greed had kept him hanging around, hoping for customers. Unwanted books piled on the tables. "You OK, Tarek?" asked John.

"No," I answered. "I lost my girlfriend, failed my exams… nothing's OK."

"Stop whining, Tarek, and while you're at it you should stop drinking as well. You can't handle it, not like me. Things could be worse."

"How could they be worse?"

And then John said, "How long have you been buying and reading all this stuff from me? Years. Didn't you learn anything? You're always saying what a great bloke you think Tom Paine was. He was too." John picked up from the table a dog-eared copy of "The Rights of Man." He held it under my nose, saying, "Tom spent his life running from the hangman and dodging the guillotine. And it didn't worry him at all. He just carried on. Challenging tyrants and despots. So stop whinging and whining, Tarek, and get on with your life. Everything will work out—and now clear off."

I walked around the corner and came to the observatory where my old friend Cem had told me that time when we were kids about the asteroid hurtling towards the earth and how it would be the Americans that would save us and not the Turks or the Germans. Further down the road, I reached the Marriot Hotel and asked myself how many thousands of people must have spent the night there since the time when Mo, The Little Sheikh, had spent the last weeks of his life there. Crossing the road to the Trade Tower, I felt as usual the strong gust of wind between the two tall buildings. I looked up at the obelisk and its pyramid on top with The All-Seeing Eye, which caused so much fear and loathing amongst the Illuminati and Freemason hating, anti-Semitic Muslim friends of my father. It stood as usual, ruling over the evil city of Frankfurt, city of banks and money and greed.

I kept on walking along the road to the railway station, and I could see from a distance the taxi ranks. I recognized a couple of colleagues of my father. I could see Jabbar as well, my Afghan school buddy, the honor-killing specialist who also drove a taxi now. He seemed to be arguing with some of the older guys. Things don't change I guess. The Middle East conflict were still being acted out by Frankfurt taxi drivers. As I came closer I saw my father get out of his cab. Since the divorce I'd seen him rarely. I went up to him. He'd gotten old. There were crow's feet under his eyes and a lot of grey in his beard.

"Your mom told me on the phone about your exam and everything." He looked at me thoughtfully: "Maybe you and I never really understood each other, there were other influences I guess, but I think in a way we're pretty much the same. If you need a job, maybe wanna drive a taxi, I could put in a word for you, help you with the test." We waved goodbye and I walked on towards the station entrance.

Then suddenly I heard a shout and looked across the street to the top of the Kaiser Straße, where hundreds of junkies gathered everyday, drinking and dealing and waiting for the man. And in the middle of them I saw two men the same age as me with shaved heads and muscular bodies. They were drunk and raising their hands in Nazi salutes and shouting at passersby: "Deutschland! Deutschland!" It were the Gauland Twins. To an African-looking couple, they bellowed: "Showers to the right!" And to one of the junkie's dogs who had come across and started barking at them, they raised their arms and shouted: "Heil Hitler!" The Gaulands hadn't changed either—they had just gotten more rotten and numerous.

I walked into the crowded Friday evening railway station. Commuters and travelers were rushing around, getting away for the weekend. Everyone had a life. I walked towards the Carminez Coffee Shop. It had a huge, open front directed onto the concourse of the station. I could see them all already from a distance, sitting there. Hannah, Osman, and Jusra, and two other of my former student friends, a guy called Jens (a real slime-ball) and a girl called Helena (a real nasty piece of work). They were all wearing their business clothes, and with their laptops and aluminum briefcases, looked the epitome of young professionals enjoying a preweekend drink. For a moment I hesitated. Should I go in? How will they react? They must all know by now that I'd failed. I was ashamed to present myself to them. But I took a deep breath and walked across. Jens saw me first and whispered something to the others. They looked up in my direction. Their expressions were a mix of mingled surprise and sneering. Hannah quickly gathered up her stuff and disappeared before I arrived. It was like a knife in my back. As I arrived at their table Jens and Helena stood up and left. Helena walked by without even looking at me, and Jens gave me a quick, despising grin. Ice cold. Like I was a leper to them or something. Not even worth a hello. Osman and Jusra remained sitting at their table. I stood in front of them and said, "Hi."

"Hi, Tarek," said Jusra, "and how are things?"

"Not so good."

"Oh my," said Osman. "What on earth has happened?" They knew already. The pair of them could hardly contain their smirks.
"I failed the exam."

Osman looked me directly in the eyes: "What else did you expect, Tarek?" he asked, raising his eyebrows. Then he stood up, saying to Jusra, "I'll fetch the car."

"I'll come with you," said Jusra, and followed her husband. Suddenly, she turned around a couple of feet away from me and hissed: "Tarek, I knew you would never amount to anything," and walked after her husband. I stood alone at the table, half-empty coffee cups in front of me. I watched them leaving the cafe. Between them and the door was a North African cleaning lady wearing a head scarf, who was mopping the floor. They both walked straight across the floor she was cleaning, so close to her that she had to pull the mop back quickly and stop working. I saw her annoyed expression. They'd walked across her clean, wet floor without even giving their Muslim sister a glance.
I just stood there for a long time. The whole thing had been a disaster. It couldn't have gone worse. Hannah leaving like she did and the sneers and insinuations of the others had been bad enough, but Jusra's final comment had almost destroyed me.

Like a robot, I left the cafe and in a kind of trance and wandered through the station, here and there, no direction at all. I ended up standing at a table at one of those mobile coffee stands at the head of the railway platforms. I decided to get a coffee. I had the feeling that the whole world hated me.

Here I was, 32 years of age. A failed student. Years and years had gone by for nothing. I was a complete loser, just standing there with empty hands. Tarek, with the big mouth and the big plans. Tarek, the clown with the big ideas. And where was I now? Everyone else was moving right along and looking back at me and thinking like Jusra: he never amounted to anything. And in that moment standing there in Frankfurt Railway Station on a Friday evening it became clear to me that everything really was over and that I would never now become a Clarence Darrow or an Atticus Finch. Just a nobody, from nowhere.

The Defense

As I was standing there looking at all the people swirling around me, I saw the young girl who was serving behind the counter. She was small, about 18 years of age, with short, cropped brown hair and a boyish appearance. But what was remarkable about her was that she was obviously afraid of something. I could see it in her face and in her body language. She kept looking around her, and even when she was serving the customers, seemed to be nervously watching the railway station behind them. I tried to work out what it was she was afraid of. It was just a normal Friday evening. If I hadn't been in such a state of depression, I wouldn't have noticed her. But I seemed to need some sort of focal point, something to hold on to in all that movement around me. Something to meditate on.

Then she saw me staring at her. She gave me a look of complete hate. And I thought, this is all I need: Hannah, Jusra, Osman, Jens and Helena, The Gaulands, Herr Dr. Adolf von Reich—the whole filthy world—lining up to despise me and now this little coffee floozie thinks she can join the queue.

Who the heck does she think she is? She have a problem with me or what? She was still staring at me.

"Everything alright with you?" I asked aggressively.

It was a challenge.

"Why shouldn't it be?" she spat back. "What's your problem?"

Doesn't she care how she talks to the customers? Or is it just me? "Listen girly, nothing's OK with me! My girlfriend dropped me, I failed my exam, ten years for nothing, and I don't even have a job. At least you've got a job, a job where you can insult people."

"You're not the only one here who's lost their girlfriend," she said bitterly.

"What do you mean?"
"What I mean? You should know," she said poisonously.

"What should I know?"

"Because you're one of them!"

"One of what?" I asked with irritation.

"A Muslim, a fanatic."

The miracle of it all was that we actually got to talking. We talked that evening. Over the next few days I got into the habit of dropping by and we talked quite a lot. She told me her name was Miriam Bloom and that she came from Offenbach, the town next to Frankfurt. She'd been working at the coffee stand for about a year. It was her first job. She also told me that when she was still in school, she'd started an affair with another girl who came from a conservative Muslim Turkish family. The family had found out about it and broken the relationship up by threatening Miriam with violence and sending their daughter back to Turkey, where she was forcibly married to an old man in the mountains, a cousin of the family. That was Miriam's first encounter with Islam. She lived for weeks in fear of the family clan.

Her second encounter with Islam was when her boss started to tell her to watch out for unattended bags and suspicious objects in or around the coffee stand. She became aware of the security measures, police officers with dogs and machine guns, which had been introduced in the railway station for fear of Islamist terrorist attacks. She began to become frightened. She read everything she could about terrorist attacks in the past in Europe and the USA. And the more she read, the greater her fear became because she realized that whereas most people simply just pass through the railway station, she had to stand there all day, and at any time a Muslim lunatic could explode a bomb. She was, she felt, a sitting target for any maniac who happened to come along. And it got worse and worse, but she needed the job.

"You know, Tarek," she said to me once. "It's easy for people to laugh at me being scared, but they only walk through here, catch a train. I am here all day long. Everyday. And if anything like a terrorist attack happens in this railway station, I'm just a sitting duck. If there is an explosion, what will I do? Hide under the counter? From the religion of peace? They say it has nothing to do with Islam. I've read all about it. Everyday. New York, Madrid, London, Paris, Cologne, Bonn, Brussels, Stockholm, Berlin, the children in Manchester… railway stations, airports, public places, and they all say it's got nothing to do with Islam… 9/11 had nothing to do with Islam, London and Paris had nothing to do with Islam, it has never had anything to do with Islam…then what does it have to with? The Jehovah's Witnesses? The Mormons? Yoga? Ice hockey? Flower arranging?" And then she told me what she was going to do, her plan. Her plan that would set her free. She almost froze the blood in my veins.

"Look out there, Tarek," she said, almost in a whisper, pointing out toward the crowds in the railway station. "One day soon, during a completely normal working day when the fear in me gets to be too much, I'm gonna turn the tables on them."

For a moment I couldn't hear her because of the loudspeakers announcing train departures, but I could see a maddened, almost insane look in her eyes.

"I am going to wait until I see a group of them, with their beards and their head scarves, standing in front of me out there. A nice big pack of them. And then I'm going to leave my little coffee stand, and I am going to walk right up to them, with one their Qurans in one hand and a cigarette lighter in the other. And then as loud as I can, I will curse their God with the foulest language I can think of: their prophet, their religion, in German, in English, so they understand. And then I will burn that Quran! Throw it among them and film it all with my phone."

I went back 16 years, to the living room in Shackleton. Paul's birthday. A Quran hurled across the room. A group of people. And the worst thing was that I knew her well enough to know that she would do it. I was standing opposite a person who was just like me…I was scared. I was scared for her.

"Look, Miriam," I said. "I can understand you being afraid. I can understand you being angry. I can understand you wanting to scream it all out. Believe me, I know where you're at. I've been there myself. But Miriam, if you do that, what do you think will happen? The consequences. They could tear you to death. Kill you on the spot. The police would arrest you anyway. There are laws against blasphemy. Against insult. I studied law, for God's sake. They'll bang you up in jail, that's what they'll do. No, they'll say you're insane and put you in the funny farm. The madhouse. You want to go to Niederrad? Is this what you want, Miriam? And no one will care at all. They will say it was just a crazy, stupid girl screaming in the railway station. It won't even make the news because no one wants any trouble. And Miriam, are you sure you've thought this thing through? I mean, how are you going to burn…I mean how, could you please explain, how are you going to burn a thick Quran with a lighter and film at the same time? Hold the camera with your teeth or something?"

Miriam laughed, despite herself.

Thank you, Sally!

It looked like I managed to calm her down. All I wanted to do was prevent her from doing the same type of dumb action that I had done in Shackleton. Something she'd regret all her life. Something that would ruin her life. Like Shackleton. We stood there in silence. The tumult of the railway station around us. And then I had the great idea. The truly great idea. Perhaps the greatest idea I'd had in my whole useless life. There was a sign above her head on the coffee stand which I hadn't noticed before. It said, "Male or Female Help Sought. Experience unnecessary. Full or part time." And then I asked her, "Hey Miriam, your company still looking for people? They need someone here?"

"Yeah," she said. "They want to build the stand up a bit, couple more machines, gonna need two people."

"OK," I said. "I'll apply for the job."

"You? Here? What's the point of that?" she asked, surprised.

"Four eyes are better then two. If there are two of us here watching, and some Muslim loony comes sneaking up with a bomb in a suitcase, he'll have no chance at all." All I wanted to do was protect her. To defend her. "I look after you. You look after me. We both look after Frankfurt. Deal?"

I could see that Miriam was a bit embarrassed by the whole thing, but at the same time seemed to have calmed down and was somehow happier, somehow relieved. And the next day I had the job. I was working there five days a week, and it wasn't a bad job. Kept my mind off other things. Miriam could be a lot of fun to work with. But of course, one day, it had to happen. Hannah with her Trojan

Muslims came by, and a couple of other familiar faces. They all saw me selling coffee next to Miriam, and walking by, started to giggle. One of them said, "Look at Tarek, what a loser, selling donuts." They walked on, laughing and looking back with sneers on their faces. And do you know what? This time, it didn't matter to me at all! I didn't care what they thought because I knew something that they didn't. Something that they could never know. All they could see was me selling coffee and donuts. What they could never know was that I was defending my client, Miriam Rebecca Bloom, in this case actually preventing her from committing a crime in advance. I, Tarek Waleed, (bar exam failed) had taken criminal defense to a completely different level. I was conducting an invisible defense in the middle of a German railway station far beyond the orthodox legal world of barren court rooms, boring legal clauses, and frozen, dull procedures. It didn't matter what Hannah or Osman or Jusra or Jens or Helena or Dr. Adolf von Reich thought of me, and what they would say about me from one end of Frankfurt to the other. I was free of them. Free for all of time.

Atticus Finch and Clarence Darrow did it for other people, Paul and Heather Miller did it for me, and now chance had given me the possibility, despite my failing, to qualify to act as a sort of invisible lawyer, a shady lawyer in the best possible sense of the word, and prevent a disturbed young woman from destroying her life. Suddenly I had the feeling that at last I had found the ability in myself to give something to other people to protect them, even when necessary, like Paul was able to do for me when I was out of line in Shackleton. I wasn't just acting for myself, a spoiled, selfish kid. Shackleton had made me. It had taken a long time. Paul and Heather had made me. Now it had come out. After all these years I realized what Paul had taught me: to take responsibility for another human being regardless of cost.

Over the days and weeks while we worked together I noticed that

Miriam was becoming less afraid and less paranoid about the people around her. Her hate had diminished and she had even begun a relationship with a girl she had met. She seemed to be becoming happy. And in my own case, I had the feeling that spoiled, selfish Tarek had become another person. I was all grown up now, a mature person. I had a little common sense, I cared about the rights of man, and I had the feeling that at long last I had attained The Age of Reason.

Midnight Call to Georgia

And that is why, 16 years after the event, I finally felt strong enough—man enough—to call Paul and Heather.

It's approaching midnight in Frankfurt, and I'm sitting in my room in Bockenheim. It's quiet. All by myself. The room where I have always lived. And the whole time I'm looking at the telephone because I know that in 10 minutes I am going to call Paul and Heather. And I'll be telling them how it was only in the last few days that I have come to realize what they set in motion in me and to thank them for it. My heart is beating strongly. I'm nervous. I've got to get this right. I turn and face the mirror behind me. I've got to rehearse this. What I am going to say? I go through it over and over again:

"Hi Paul, this is Tarek…do you remember me?…I should have made this call 16 years ago on 9/11, … but I didn't have the guts. I was too shocked, too ashamed. Maybe I don't have the right to call you like this, maybe it's inappropriate, but I'm doing it anyway because I want to apologize to you, Paul, and to Heather for what I did and said and how I was back then. In a way, maybe it's better that it has taken so long, because if I'd called back then it would have simply been an apology. But now it's much more than that. It's a thank you. It's a heartfelt thank you to you both. I am saying this in the awareness that I have grown because of you and through the seed that you and Heather planted in me. They have now borne fruit, things I didn't understand back then. Maybe it's hard for you both to understand, but it was only today, this very day, that I've come to realize that what I've been doing here in Frankfurt in the last couple of weeks and all the years and months of reading and thinking that led up to it all, was the completion of a journey that you set me on back then, when I was just a dumb, spoiled kid in your home in Shackleton.

It's hard to believe, …but I have managed to take responsibility for another human being just because it was right to do so. Just like both of you did for me. I now understand that you were both the embodiment of the values and virtues of your land. Because your country, the USA, takes responsibility as well and ensures, with its fundamental values of the Anglo-American democratic tradition formed all those years ago by your Founding Fathers, that we today enjoy some sort of halfway decent world. Without those ideas of the Founding Fathers, we here in Europe and in many other areas of the world would either be Nazi or Stalinist or in a religious Stone Age. It is the ideas of Benjamin Franklin, Thomas Jefferson, Tom Paine, and the other Founding Fathers of the USA that have prevented this. This I believe with every fiber of my being. All that is positive in the world is down to those guys: their ideas of the equality of men, the rights of human beings, freedom of speech, the pursuit of happiness, democratic government, and the right to live in freedom have made the world a better place.

We all make mistakes; governments and people make mistakes, but the American people have the advantage that if they slip into error, they always have that bedrock of belief and thought laid down by the founders of their nation that they can refer back to, use as a compass. Which other countries have that? Government of the people, by the people, for the people.

Here in Europe and elsewhere it is chic and fashionable to blame America for everything, for all the misery in the world. Whatever happens, America is to blame. What a pack of spoiled brats we are. Nothing better to do than stomp our foot, defying daddy. Whatever comes out of the US—be it political, scientific, technological, cultural—is lapped up, digested, enjoyed, and then by way of thanks denigrated. Just like me in Shackleton. We enjoy their protection and support, and claim they are only doing it for their own evil ends. But without them there would be just one form of tyranny or another in the world. Yes, the whole world loves to laugh at you and criticize you, but all the time knowing, deep down in our hypocritical beings, that we need someone like Gary Cooper in High Noon who is doing the heavy lifting that no one else has the guts or ability to do. The Founding Fathers had this in their DNA. I don't see it here, in Europe. When I walk along streets in Germany today, I see these brass shields embedded here and there in the sidewalk outside houses where Jewish people used to live in the Nazi time. They document the names of the people, their ages, and to which place they were deported to. This is all very well meant post-factum, but I always look at the houses around and ask myself, 'Where were the neighbors?' If it had happened in Shackleton, someone coming in the middle of the night to take your Jewish neighbors away, I know that you and Heather would be out on the street with a shotgun in one hand and Thoreau's 'Civil Disobedience' in the other…

And like you told me that time, Paul, the great Tom Paine once said, 'These are the times that try men's souls…' and here in Europe, the demagogues of the right, and the religious fascists, are on the march once more. As if we had learned nothing. Houston, we have a problem. Is this what thousands of young Americans and British soldiers died on the beaches of Normandy 70 years ago for? That we should go back to Nazism and religious madness like dogs to our vomit. I've had it with these European Sunshine Democrats. Their apparent democracy is only skindeep, not seated in the bone marrow like yours. Here, extremism or total indifference is the order of the day. With you, it is true commitment, long-term. The Anglosphere is the true mother and sustainer of freedom and human rights. In the course of my life, I think I have been exposed to all sorts of –isms: Islamism, Fascism, Antisemitism, Anti-Americanism, and all sorts of extremism. I have chosen democracy, the real thing, the democracy of the American Founding Fathers…

Ok, Paul, so maybe I sound like a fanatic to you. Maybe it's in my nature. My father was a fanatic before me. I guess you can say Tom Paine was a fanatic as well. It just depends on what you're fanatic about, I think. I guess you can say I've become a fanatic for democracy. I don't see anything wrong in that—for the life of me, I don't…I've got you and Heather to thank for this, Paul. By your example, you told me how to live and you even showed me the books I could read. I even reconstructed your library here in Frankfurt, the best I could…All I can say is, 'Thank you, forever.' That's all I wanted to say."

It's midnight. My heart is beating like mad. My hands are shaking. I reach across, pick up my phone, and dial the Miller's number. It's been 16 years. I hear a voice on the other end.

"Hi Paul? Heather? This is Tarek…do you remember me?"